James Mercer Garnett

Beowulf

An Anglo-Saxon Poem. The Fight at Finnsburg. Third Edition

James Mercer Garnett

Beowulf

An Anglo-Saxon Poem. The Fight at Finnsburg. Third Edition

ISBN/EAN: 9783744764896

Printed in Europe, USA, Canada, Australia, Japan

Cover: Foto ©Andreas Hilbeck / pixelio.de

More available books at **www.hansebooks.com**

... þcan áriht ... ...

de feorran cumene ofer geofenes
gang geata leode. þone yldestan o[retmecgas]
mecgas. beowulf nemnað. hy benan
synt þ hie þeoden min wið þe moton
word[um] wrixlan noðu him wearne
ge teoh ðinra gegn cwida glædma
hroð gar. hy on wig ge tawum wyrðe
þinceað. eorla ge æhtlan huru se
aldor deah se þæm heaðo rincum
hider wisade.

·VI·

hroð gar maþelode helm scyldinga
ic hine cuðe cniht wesende. wæs hi[s]
eald fæder. ecg þeo haten ðæm to ha[m]
for geaf hreþel geata angan dohtor
is his eaforan nu heard her cumen
sohte holdne wine. ðonne sægdon þ
sæliþende þaðe gif sceattas geata
fyre don hyder to þance þ he ...

138ᵃ to his wine driht ne her sýndon ge*fere*
de feorran cumene ofer geofenes be
gang geata leode þone ýldestan ore*t*
mecgas . beowulf nemnað hý benan
sýnt þ̄ hie þeoden min wið þe moton
wordum wrixlan noðu him wearne
geteoh ðinra gegn cwida glaedman
hroðgar hý onwig getawum wýrðe
þinceað . eorla geaehtlan huru se
aldor deah se þaem heaðo rincum
hider wisade .

· VI ·

Hroðgar maþelode helm scýldinga
ic hine cuðe cniht wesende waes his
ealdfaeder ecgþeo haten ðaem to hā
forgeaf hreþel geata angan dohtor
is his eaforan nu heard her eumen
sohte holdne wine . ðonne saegdon þ̄
saeliþende þaðe gif sceattas geata
fýre don þýder to þance þ̄ he ·xxx·

———————————

Transliteration of Facsimile of fol. 138ᵃ Ms. Cotton. Vitellius A XV
in the British Museum.

BEOWULF:

An Anglo-Saxon Poem,

AND

THE FIGHT AT FINNSBURG.

TRANSLATED BY

JAMES M. GARNETT, M.A., LL.D.,

PROFESSOR OF THE ENGLISH LANGUAGE AND LITERATURE IN THE
UNIVERSITY OF VIRGINIA; TRANSLATOR OF "ELENE"
AND OTHER ANGLO-SAXON POEMS.

*With Facsimile of the Unique Manuscript in the British
Museum, Cotton. Vitellius A XV.*

THIRD EDITION.

BOSTON, U.S.A.:
GINN & COMPANY, PUBLISHERS.
1895.

To my Wife.

CONTENTS.

BEOWULF AND GRENDEL.

I.

BEOWULF AND THE DRAGON.

THE FIGHT AT FINNSBURG.

PREFACE.

DURING the session of 1878–79, while reading "Beowulf" with a post-graduate class at St. John's College, Annapolis, Md., I made a line-for-line translation of the poem for my own use. In reading the poem I used Grein's text of his separate edition (1867), and carefully collated with it the editions of Kemble (1835), Thorpe (1855), Arnold (1876), and Heyne (3d ed., 1873), which last was in the hands of the class. When the publication of this translation was recently suggested and approved by scholars in whom I had confidence, I revised it carefully, and gave it as nearly as possible a rhythmical form, still retaining the line-for-line feature. This involves naturally much inversion and occasional obscurity, and lacks smoothness; but it seemed to me to give the general reader a better idea of the poem than a mere prose translation would do, in addition to the advantage of literalness. While it would have been easy, by means of periphrasis and freer translation, to mend some of the defects chargeable to the line-for-line form, the translation would have lacked literalness, which I regarded as the most important object. I retained Grein's text, but have added Notes giving a translation of the variations in the text of Heyne's fourth edition (1879), both on account of its importance as the latest critical text, and the fact that it has just been republished in this country,

edited by Professor James A. Harrison, of Washington
and Lee University, Lexington, Virginia, so that the
Anglo-Saxon text is now easily accessible in inexpensive
form.   I retained also Grein's divisions of the poem, and
have added headings giving the contents of each division.
I felt very much the want of an Anglo-Saxon dictionary,
— the new edition of Bosworth, edited by Professor
Toller, of Owens College, Manchester, not yet having
been issued, — and I was, therefore, entirely dependent
on the German ·glossaries of Grein and Heyne, which
have been my constant companions.   Their translations
have also been referred to, especially in difficult passages ;
but often they do not suit the editions used, as Grein's
translation was made from the text in his *Bibliothek der
A. S. Poesie* (1857), and Heyne's from that in his *first*
edition (1863), both of which vary frequently and mate-
rially from the later texts of these writers.   I have carefully avoided using any English translation.   In respect
to the rhythmical form, I have endeavored to preserve
two accents to each half-line, with cæsura, and while
not seeking alliteration, have employed it purposely
wherever it readily presented itself.   I considered that it
mattered little whether the feet were iambi or trochees,
anapæsts or dactyls, the preservation of the two accents
being the main point, and have freely made use of all the
usual licenses in Early English verse, which are enumer-
ated and discussed at length by Schipper in his recent
excellent work on Old-English Metre.   To attain this
point, I have sometimes found it necessary to place
unemphatic words in accented positions, and words

usually accented in unaccented ones, which licenses can also be found in Early English verse. Illustrations of these rhythmical features might be adduced, but it would unnecessarily prolong this Preface, and the reader will discover them for himself. While the reader of modern English verse may sometimes be offended by the rugged-ness of the rhythm, it is hoped the Anglo-Saxon scholar will make allowances for the difficulty of reproducing, even approximately, the rhythm of the original. The reproduction of the sense as closely as possible had to be kept constantly in view, even to the detriment of the smoothness of the rhythm. In the Introduction I have endeavored to give the general reader some idea of the poem, although with greater brevity than I could have wished; and to further this end I have translated, with abridgment and a few additions, the Glossary of Proper Names appended to Heyne's edition. A few of the Notes are also explanatory, and I have usually followed Heyne in his interpretations, although where he and Grein differ I have given both views. The question of the composi-tion of the poem is by no means a settled one, but it could be barely touched upon in a brief Introduction. Criticism of the text belongs rather to the editor than to the translator, and in important passages I have generally referred the reader to Heyne's notes. I have thought it advisable to add as full a Bibliography as the materials at hand for its compilation permitted; but as I cannot flatter myself that it is complete, I shall be glad to be informed of any omissions noticed. If I have contributed in any respect to bring before the general public a knowledge of this most ancient and most important of Anglo-Saxon poems, and to create among English-speaking people a desire for further acquaintance with our earliest literature, I shall be abundantly satisfied.

My thanks are due to Mr. F. J. Furnivall, Director of the Early English Text Society, for permission to publish a facsimile page of the manuscript from the autotypes of the Society's forthcoming edition ;* to Professor Francis A. March, of Easton, Pa., for some additions to the Bibliography ; and to Dr. William Hand Browne, Librarian of the Johns Hopkins University, Baltimore, for affording me every facility in the use of the Library, and for kindly reading over a large portion of the translation.

J. M. GARNETT.

GARNETT's UNIVERSITY SCHOOL,
  ELLICOTT CITY, MARYLAND.
      August, 1882.

* This facsimile has been reduced to suit the page, so that the letters are smaller than in the original Ms.

PREFACE TO THE SECOND EDITION.

In preparing for the press this edition, I have carefully compared the translation with Professor Wülcker's
critical text in the first volume of his edition of Grein's
Bibliothek der A. S. Poesie, and, wherever necessary,
with the Facsimile of the Manuscript, edited by Professor
Zupitza for the Early English Text Society, both works
having appeared since the publication of my first edition.
Wherever Wülcker differs from Grein I have added notes
showing the variations, and I have also supplied omissions in the notes of variations from Grein in the text
or explanations of Heyne's fourth edition. Were this
translation designed *solely* for the general reader, the
expenditure of time and labor which the preparation of
the notes involved would have been entirely unnecessary ;
but, as it is intended also for the aid of students of the
poem, I hope that this regard for their interests may not
have been mistaken. I have revised certain passages
with a view to greater accuracy, but I have not changed
the plan of the work, for that would have necessitated
the re-writing of the whole translation. The Anglo-Saxon
inversions easily become familiar after a little reading,
notwithstanding the difference from the usual English
order. I was happy to find the plan of a line-for-line
translation approved by a distinguished scholar whose

judgment I value highly, and whose reputation embraces both sides of the water. He writes: "I think your idea of the kind of translation desirable is entirely right, and you have carried it out with no wrenching of the modern dialect to suit the old." While it is not so acceptable to the general reader as a freer and smoother version would be, I still think that it will be more serviceable to students, and the exhaustion of the first edition within two years from the date of publication has served to confirm this opinion. I have made some additions to the Bibliography, and have noted in it certain reviews of the first edition; from some of these I have derived assistance, for which I desire to express here my obligations to the writers.

J. M. GARNETT.

University of Virginia, Va.
January, 1885.

PREFACE TO THE THIRD EDITION.

As the second edition of my translation of " Beowulf" has been out of print for over two years, and constant occupation has prevented me from giving the text any further revision, if any is needed, I have determined to issue at once the third edition to meet an immediate demand, and have inserted, with some additions, the bibliographical titles that I have collected during the past few years, which were printed separately in 1890, for distribution with reprints of the second edition. The full bibliographies that appear annually in the *Jahresbericht über die Erscheinungen auf dem Gebiete der germanischen Philologie* and in the *Anglia*, and the prospective translation of Wülker's well-known and excellent *Grundriss zur Geschichte der angelsächsischen Litteratur*, with additions, will enable the student of " Beowulf " to keep up with the literature of the subject.

It is highly probable that some titles are omitted from this list which should have been inserted. If any such are noticed by " Beowulf "-students, I shall be much obliged for the information, with full statement of title and reference. I desire to make this bibliography as complete as possible to date. I shall also be obliged for information as to any revision of the text that scholars

may think desirable, and it will receive attention hereafter. As to rhythmical revision, which some have desired,
that would not be possible without a re-writing of the
whole and a re-casting of the plates, and that I cannot
undertake. The translation has met with a much more
favorable reception than I anticipated, and if another
edition is called for, I hope to improve it further.

I am again indebted to the former Librarian of the
Johns Hopkins University, Professor William Hand
Browne, and his assistant, Mr. H. C. F. Miller, for
courteous attention in facilitating access to the excellent collection of German and English periodicals in
the Library of that University.

JAMES M. GARNETT.

University of Virginia, Va.,
    November, 1891.

INTRODUCTION.

THE Anglo-Saxon poem "Beowulf" needs no introduction to the student of English literature, but the general reader may desire some information about it as an aid to an intelligent interest in a translation of the poem.

Contents.—Its subject is, in brief, the contest of Beowulf the Geat, the hero of the poem, with the monster Grendel, and afterwards with Grendel's mother, and many years later with the fire-dragon, whom he slays, but perishes in the fight. More fully, it consists of an introduction giving some account of the genealogy of Hrothgar the Dane, and of his building the great hall Heorot, which. Grendel soon visits by night, and he devours whoever ventures to rest therein. This lasts for twelve years, until Beowulf the Geat, the thane of Hygelac, and the strongest of men, hears of it, and comes to try his strength with Grendel. His arrival by sea, introduction to Hrothgar, and their talk, are narrated at length. When all retire, Beowulf and his companions occupy the hall. Grendel soon comes and devours one, but finds his match in Beowulf. Weapons are useless against the monster, so, by main strength, Beowulf wrenches Grendel's arm from the socket, and he flees to the fen. In the morning great was the rejoicing in Heorot; feasting, horse-racing, the song of the *scop* (minstrel), mutual congratulations, and presents of Hrothgar and his wife Wealhtheow to Beowulf occupy the time. But the rejoicing was premature, for that night comes Grendel's mother to avenge her son, and carries off from the hall Aeschere, Hrothgar's counsellor. Mourning was renewed in the morning, and Beowulf, who had slept elsewhere, is sent for at once, and determines to go to the mere in search of the monster. He plunges into the water and descends to her abode, where a violent struggle ensues. Beowulf's sword is useless, but he finds in the submarine chamber an old sword of the giants, with which he despatches the monster, and returns, bringing with him Grendel's head and the hilt of the sword, the blade having melted from the poisonous blood. There is more rejoicing in Heorot, and much talk as before, with more presents. Soon after, Beowulf takes his leave and returns to the court of Hygelac, where he is welcomed at length, and shares his presents with Hygelac and his wife Hygd.

Here occurs a long intermission. Hygelac and his son Heardred are dead, and Beowulf has ascended the throne and reigned fifty winters. The hoard of a dragon is robbed by a fugitive from his master, and the dragon takes terrible vengeance on the land, vomiting fire and consuming everything, even Beowulf's palace. Beowulf resolves to risk the contest, and goes with companions to the fire-dragon's haunt. After a long speech he opens the fight, but his companions flee, all except his kinsman Wiglaf, and they two contend alone. The struggle is prolonged, and Beowulf is wounded, but the dragon is finally killed. Wiglaf brings treasures from the hoard for Beowulf to view before he dies, for the dragon's bite is deadly poison. Beowulf charges Wiglaf to build him a mound on the Whale's ness, and breathes his last. Wiglaf upbraids the thanes for their cowardice, and sends a messenger to his other comrades, who makes a long speech on the occasion. They join Wiglaf, inspect the treasure, commit Beowulf's body to the funeral-pyre, and erect a mound, in which the treasures are buried, in honor of their king.

The above is a brief summary of the poem, but numerous episodes are introduced, chiefly in the speeches, though some in the narrative, which make considerable digressions, and interrupt the action of the poem. It is sometimes difficult, too, to see their connection, and to frame a consistent account of personages and events, to which often the merest allusion is made ; but the editors, especially Grein and Heyne, have been very successful in their elucidation of obscure points.

Date. — The poem is preserved in but one manuscript (Cotton. Vitellius A XV) in the British Museum, which, according to palæographers, dates from the tenth century, ~ but the composition of the poem is much earlier. The allusions on which the approximate date of the poem is based are two, namely: to the death of Hygelac, who has been identified by Outzen and Leo with the Chochilaicus, (or -lagus), mentioned by Gregory of Tours, and in the Gesta Regum Francorum, who is said to have been killed in a battle with the Franks in A.D. 511–12, which date supplies the *terminus a quo ;* and the mention of the Merovingians (l. 2921), not later then than A.D. 752, which gives the *terminus ad quem.* Allowing for the reigns of Heardred and Beowulf, if historical personages, and the lapse of time for mythical adventures to cluster around the name of Beowulf,

and we bring down the poem to the first half of the eighth
century, though Heyne assigns it to the seventh century.

In any event, it is the oldest extant heroic poem in any
Germanic tongue, and gives the earliest representation
that we possess in the vernacular of the life of our
Teutonic forefathers in their continental homes.

Scene. — The scene is manifestly not in England, notwithstanding the ingenious efforts of Haigh, in his "Anglo-
Saxon Sagas," to vindicate an English origin for it. It is
in Denmark, probably Zealand, and south-west Sweden,
as internal evidence and the investigations of editors,
especially of Grein (in Ebert's Jahrbuch IV. 3, 260–285),
have well shown. The origin of the poem then is Scandinavian, and it is with Scandinavian tribes, manners, and
customs that we have to do.

Tribes. — The principal tribes mentioned are the Danes,
known under the various names of North-, South-, East-, and
West-Danes, Spear-Danes, Ring-Danes, and Bright-Danes,
with their king Hrothgar; the Geats, or Goths, known as
Weder-Geats or Weders, War-Geats, Sea-Geats, with their
kings Hygelac and Beowulf; the Sweons, or Swedes, with
their king Ongentheow, and his sons Onela and Ohthere;
and the Frisians, known as North-Frisians, with their king
Finn, and West-Frisians, and inhabiting the islands and
coast west of Jutland. Fuller information is given in the
"Glossary of Proper Names."

Life of the time. — Even if the poem were composed in
the first half of the eighth century, the life depicted is that
of two centuries earlier, unless the writer transfers to those
times the manners and customs of his own day. We see

the king and his *witan* (wise men), his war-comrades, or thanes, constituting his *comitatus*, and a similar body of attendants on the great nobles. The king is the ring-giver, treasure-giver, showing that he was esteemed according to his liberality. The delight of the people is in deeds of arms and of great strength; Beowulf has the strength of thirty men. Equally prominent is the delight in feasting in beer-drinking even to excess, but a relieving feature is the song of the minstrel after the feast, who relates old sagas, and celebrates the praises of by-gone heroes and even of contemporaries. The importance of the *scop* cannot be exaggerated. It is he that preserves the record of past times, of ancestral glories, whose song enlivens every banquet. The position of woman must not be overlooked. Queen Wealhtheow and her daughter Freaware are present at the feast, and it is the queen herself who carries around the mead-cup, who welcomes the hero and bestows presents upon him. The pictures of Hygd, Hildeburg, and Thrytho, with her unenviable traits of character, show also the importance and the influence of noble women in those days.

The religious tone of the work is inconsistent. The author of the introduction tells us that the Danes " Knew not the good Lord" (l. 181), but soon after Hrothgar speaks of the power of God (l. 478), and later thanks God for the victory of Beowulf. This doubtless has led Ettmüller to his view in respect to the composition of the poem, the varying views on which point must be briefly noticed.

Composition. — Müllenhoff, in Haupt's Zeitschrift für Deutsches Alterthum, XIV, 193–244, (1869), has given the result of his twenty years' study of the poem. He finds

it to consist of five parts : an introduction, 1–193, I. 194–836,
II. 837–1628, III. 1629–2199, IV. 2200–3183. I. and IV.
are two old lays by different authors ; to I. were added, prob·
ably by two different hands, a continuation II., and then the
introduction ; a third hand (A) added III., and at the same
time interpolated I. and II. to suit it ; a fourth hand (B), or
sixth in the series, added IV., and increased the whole by episodes taken from other sagas and by theologizing additions :
B is the real interpolator, and except A no other is discov-
erable. Müllenhoff's view has been subjected to a very thorough examination by Hornburg (Program of the Lyceum
at Metz, 1877), which does not seem to be as well known
as it deserves, with the result that the *Liedertheorie* is re-
jected, and but few passages regarded as interpolated. A.
Köhler, in Z. für Deutsche Philologie, II. 305–321 (1870),
discussing the introduction and the episodes of Heremod,
has spoken out for the theory. Grein, however, did not
commit himself to it, nor has Heyne done so.[1] Ettmüller,
who published the first German translation of the poem in
1840, advanced an entirely different theory, and the last
work of the veteran scholar was to publish, in a Zurich
University Program (1875),[2] his text of the poem purged
from the interpolations of the West-Saxon monk, who, he
charges, revised the work of the Angle poet, perhaps a
heathen, in order to give it a Christian tone : these exci-
sions amount to nearly 300 lines. The Angle poet sang in

---

[1] See Preface to Heyne's 4th edition, 1879. Rieger has declared for, and
Bugge against, Müllenhoff's theory.

[2] Carmen de Beóvulfi Gautarum regis rebus praeclare gestis atque interitu, quale fuerit antequam in manus interpolatoris, monachi Vestsaxonici,
inciderat. Auctore Chlodovico Ettmüllero. Turici, 1875.

his vernacular songs of the exploits of Beowulf, which had been brought to England from Scandinavia.

The English editors, Kemble and Thorpe, give no support to the theory of separate lays, but Thorpe says: "From the allusions to Christianity contained in the poem, I do not hesitate to regard it as a Christian paraphrase of a heathen Saga, and those allusions as interpolations of the paraphrast, whom I conceive to have been a native of England of Scandinavian parentage," thus resembling in principle the theory of Ettmüller. Arnold, the latest editor, merely mentions Müllenhoff's theory to reject it with scorn, but the subject is one which deserves more respectful treatment. Some of Müllenhoff's arguments from comparison of passages seem very weak, but the poem naturally falls into three divisions : the fight with Grendel, that with Grendel's mother, and that with the dragon. The first two have a close connection and need not necessarily be separated ; the third is an addition not well joined to what precedes. The several episodes may well have been separate lays incorporated by the author of the poem.

There are also probable interpolations, especially in the religious and sermonizing parts, but whether we can get at the original form of the poem by cutting out, with Ettmüller, every Christian allusion, is another matter. The Christian poet seems to have united in one whole, on the basis of Beowulf's adventures, heathen songs as sung at the feasts, and to have been inferior in poetic power to some of his heathen predecessors, for all parts of the poem are not of equal poetic merit. The limits of this Introduction will not permit a further discussion of the subject, but it is likely to prove "the Homeric question" of Anglo-Saxon scholars.

Metre. — The poem is written in the usual Anglo-Saxon alliterative metre, consisting of two half-lines separated by cæsura, which, however, are printed by Kemble, Schaldemose, Thorpe, and Grundtvig as separate lines. The normal law of alliteration is that two accented initial syllables of words in the first half-line and one in the second must begin with the same letter, if a consonant, or with vowels, as any vowel may alliterate with another. Sometimes we find only one such alliterating syllable in each half-line. The laws of Anglo-Saxon alliteration are very fully given by Schipper in his Englische Metrik (I Theil, II Abschnitt, Kap. 1), to which the reader is referred. He has well shown that each half-line contains two strongly-accented syllables, three of which usually alliterate, as above, and the rest of the syllables are unaccented; in other words he is, with Rieger, a strong advocate of the *Zweihebungstheorie* as against the *Vierhebungstheorie* of some other scholars. Morris's remark in respect to Early English verse (quoted by Schipper, p. 270), will apply here: "It is not the number of syllables, but of accents, that is essential." Beowulf, line 40,

> "*Billum and byrnum! him on bearme læg*"
> = "With bills and burnies! On his bosom lay,"

furnishes the normal form of the line, however varied it may be by the usual licenses of Anglo-Saxon and Early English verse.

Bibliography. — The Beowulf-Ms. was first mentioned by Wanley in his Catalogue of Mss., published as the second volume of Hickes's Thesaurus of Old Northern Languages, Oxford, 1705. It was much injured in the noted fire of 1731 (by which many of the Cottonian Mss. were destroyed), and some passages cannot now be deciphered; hence the resort to conjectural emendation.

Thorkelin had two copies of the Ms. made in 1786, which are now in Copenhagen, and their readings were first given in Grundtvig's edition, 1861. Thorkelin's twenty years' labor on his edition was destroyed by the British bombardment of Copenhagen in 1807, but his copies of the Ms. were saved, so he went to work again, with the aid of the counsellor Bülow, and published the first edition of the poem in 1815.

Meantime Sharon Turner, in his History of the Anglo-Saxons (1st ed. 1803), had called attention to the poem, and in his 4th edition (1823), Vol. III, Book IX, Chap. II, he gave an analysis of it, and an English translation of extracts.

Some of the titles which follow are abridged for the sake of convenience.

EDITIONS : —

Thorkelin, G. J. — De Danorum rebus gestis secul. III et IV poema Danicum dialecto Anglosaxonica. Havniae, 1815, with Latin translation.

Conybeare, J. J., in his Illustrations of Anglo-Saxon Poetry, London, 1826, gave a collation of Thorkelin's edition with the Ms., making numerous corrections, and an English blank-verse translation of certain passages, with the A.-S. text and a Latin translation of the same.

Kemble, J. M. — The Anglo-Saxon Poems of Beowulf, the Traveller's Song, and the Battle of Finnsburg. London, 1833; 2d edition, 1835-37, in two volumes, of which the second (1837) contains a complete English translation.

Schaldemose, F. — Beowulf og Scopes Widsiŏ, to Angelsaxiske Digte. Copenhagen, 1847; 2d edition, 1851. Kemble's text, with Danish translation.

Thorpe, B. — The Anglo-Saxon Poems of Beowulf, the Scôp or Gleeman's Tale, and the Fight at Finnsburg, Oxford, 1855, with English translation. Reprinted in 1875 without change.

Grein, C. W. M. — Bibliothek der Angelsächsischen Poesie, Band I. Göttingen, 1857. Beowulf, p. 255.

Grundtvig, N. F. S. — Beowulfes Beorh. Copenhagen, London, and Leipzig, 1861. Contains collation of Thorkelin's two copies of the Ms. made in 1786.

Heyne, M. — Beowulf. Paderborn, 1863; 2d ed., 1868; 3d ed., 1873; 4th ed., 1879. Contains the best Glossary. 4th ed. makes use of Kölbing's collation of the Ms. Reviewed by Gering in Z. f. d. Phil. XII, 122; and by Brenner in Englische Studien, IV, 135, 1881, who favors consistent spelling.

Grein, C. W. M. — Beowulf nebst den Fragmenten Finnsburg und Waldere. Cassel und Göttingen, 1867.

Ettmüller, L. — Carmen de Beóvulfi Gautarum regis rebus praeclare gestis atque interitu, quale fuerit antequam in manus interpolatoris, monachi Vestsaxonici, inciderat. Turici, 1875. Reviewed by Suchier in Jenaer Literaturzeitung, No. 47, 1876; and by Schönbach in Z. f. d. Alt., XXI, Anzeiger III, 1877.

Arnold, Thomas. — Beowulf. A heroic poem of the eighth century, London, 1876, with English translation. Reviewed in Athenaeum, July to Dec., 1877, p. 862; by Sweet in Academy, Vol. XI; in Liter. Centr., 1877, No. 20; and by Wülcker in Anglia, I, 177, who finds much blameworthy.

Wülcker, R. P. — Grein's Bibliothek der A. S. Poesie. Neu bearbeitet, u.s.w. I Band. 1te Hälfte. Kassel, 1881. Text nach der Handschrift. Restored text, with critical notes, in I Band, 2 te Hälfte. Kassel, 1883.

Holder, A. — Beowulf. I. Abdruck der Handschrift. 2 te Auflage. Freiburg u. Tübingen, 1882. In Germanischer Bücherschatz. Ms. collated by Holder in 1875, with use of Thorpe's original collation in 1830. II. Text and Glossary, 1884.

Harrison, J. A., and *Sharp, R.* — Beowulf. With text and glossary, on the basis of M. Heyne. Boston: Ginn, Heath, & Co., 1883. Heyne's notes omitted.

The Early English Text Society has now published, under the editorship of Professor J. Zupitza, of Berlin, a Facsimile of the entire Beowulf-Manuscript. No. 77. London, 1882.

TRANSLATIONS. In addition to translations with the editions mentioned above, separate translations, some of them only partial, have been published as follows : —

Grundtvig, N. F. S. — Bjowulfs Drape. Copenhagen, 1820; 2d edition, 1865. Reviewed by J. Grimm in Gött. Anzeiger, 1823.
Leo, II. — Ueber Beowulf. Halle, 1839. Extracts translated.
Ettmüller, L. — Beowulf. Stabreimend übersetzt. Zürich, 1840
Wackerbarth, A. D. — Beowulf, translated into English verse. London, 1849. Irregular measures.
Grein, C. W. M. — Dichtungen der Angelsachsen, stabreimend übersetzt. 2 Bde. Göttingen, 1857-59. I Band. 2 te Ausgabe, 1863. Beowulf, p. 222. Not suited to his separate ed. in some passages owing to change of text. 2d ed. by Wülcker, 1883.
Sandras, G. S. — De carminibus Caedmoni adjudicatis. Paris, 1859. Contains extract from Beowulf, with Latin translation.
Simrock, K. — Beowulf. Uebersetzt u. erläutert. Stuttgart u. Augsburg, 1859. Preserves alliteration.
Heyne, M. — Paderborn, 1863. In iambic verses. Will not suit his 4th edition in some passages owing to change of text.
Von Wolzogen, H. — Beowulf. Aus dem Angelsächsischen. Leipzig, n.d. (1873?). Preserves alliteration.
Botkine, L. — Beowulf. Epopée Anglo-Saxonne. Traduite en français pour la première fois. Havre, 1877. Prose, with passages occasionally omitted. Reviewed by Körner in Englische Studien, II, 248, 1879, who proposes emendations.
Lumsden, H. W. — Beowulf, translated into modern rhymes. London, 1881. Ballad-measure used, and passages occasionally omitted. Reviewed in Athenæum, Jan. to June, 1881, p. 587; Academy, Vol. XIX; by Garnett, J. M., in Amer. Jour. of Philology, II, 355; and by Wülcker in Anglia, Anz. IV, 69. Second edition, revised and corrected, 1883.

GENERAL WORKS, ESSAYS, DISSERTATIONS, AND MAGAZINE ARTICLES : —

Kemble, J. M. — Ueber die Stammtafel der Westsachsen. Munich, 1836. Reviewed by J. Grimm in Götting. Anzeiger, 1836.
Grundtvig, N. F. S., — in Barfods Brage og Idun, IV, 481. (1841.)
Haigh, D. H. — The Anglo-Saxon Sagas. London, 1861. Attempts to find in England the places mentioned in Beowulf.
Heyne, M. — Ueber die Halle Heorot. Paderborn, 1864.

Botkine, L. — Beowulf. Analyse historique et géographique. Paris, 1876. Replaced by the introduction to his translation. Reviewed by Körner in Englische Studien, I, 495.

Dederich, H. — Hist. u. geogr. Studien zum A. S. Beówulfliede. Köln, 1877. Follows Müllenhoff. Reviewed by Müllenhoff in Z. für d. Alterthum (Neue Folge, IX. 3), XXI, Anzeiger III; by Suchier in Jenaer Literaturzeitung, No. 47, 1876; and by Körner in Englische Studien, I, 481. See also Revue Critique, No. 52, 1876.

Hornburg. — Die Composition des Beowulf. Program of the Lyceum in Metz, 1877. Opposes Müllenhoff. Reviewed by Hummel in Herrig's Archiv, LXII, 231.

Nader, E. — Zur Syntax des Beowulf. Two Programs of the Staats-Ober-Realschule in Brünn, 1879-80. Reviewed by Bernhardt in Literaturblatt für germ. u. rom. Philologie, 1880, p.439.

Schubert. — De Anglosaxonum arte metrica. Berol., 1870. Opposed in his Göttingen Dissertation by

Vetter, F. — Ueber die Germanische Alliterationspoesie. Vienna, 1872; and Zum Muspilli, u.s.w. Vienna, 1872.

Rehrmann. — Essay on Anglo-Saxon Poetry. Program of the Höhere Bürgerschule in Lübben, 1876.

Rieger, M. — Die Alt- u. Angel-sächsische Verskunst. Halle, 1876, and in Z. für d. Philologie, VII. 1. (1876.)

Schipper, J. — Englische Metrik. I Theil. Altenglische Metrik. Bonn, 1882. Section II treats the Anglo-Saxon Period.

Grein, C. W. M. — Die historischen Verhältnisse des Beowulfliedes. Ebert's Jahrbuch für rom. und engl. Literatur, IV, 260, (1862). Standard authority.

Kölbing, E. — Zur Beowulf-handschrift. Herrig's Archiv für das studium der neueren sprachen, LVI, 91, (1876). Complete collation of the Ms. Sievers and Zupitza have also collated the Ms.

Schultze, M. — Ueber das Beowulfslied. Program of Realschule at Elbing, 1864. Contents noted in Herrig's Archiv, XXXVII, 232.

Schultze, M. — Altheidnisches in der A. S. poesie, speciell im Beowulfsliede. Berlin, 1877. See Revue Critique, 1877, No. 82; and Ausland, No. 31.

Cosijn, P. J. — Beowulf. Taalkundige Bijdragen, I, 286.

Schröder, L. — Om Bjowulfs-drapen. Copenhagen, 1875.

Arnheim, Dr. — Ueber das Beowulflied. Bericht über die Jacobsonsche Schule zu Seesen, 1867-71.

Müller, N. — Die mythen des Beowulf in ihrem verhältniss zur germ. mythologie betrachtet. Deutsche Studienblätter von Roltsch, III, 13 and 14.

Kölbing, E. — Kleine Beiträge. Kölbing's Englische Studien, III, 92; zu Beowulf, 168.

Suchier, H. — Ueber die Sage von Offa und Thrytho. Paul und Braune's Beitraege, IV. 500.

Skeat, W. W. — The Name Beowulf. Academy, 1877, I. 163.

Bugge, S. — Til de oldengelske digte om Beowulf og Waldere. Tidskrift for Philologi og Pädagogik, VIII. 40 and 287, 1869-70.

Vigfusson, G. — Grettis Saga, in Prolegomena to his Sturlunga Saga (2 vols. Oxford, 1878) I. p. xlviii, and in Icelandic Prose Reader (Oxford, 1879), pp. 200 and 404.

Gering, H. — Der Beówulf und die Isländische Grettissaga, in Anglia, III. 74 (1880).

Smith, C. Sprague. — Beowulf Gretti, in New Englander IV. 49 (Jan. 1881).

Ettmüller, L. — Altnordischer Sagenschatz. 1870.

Heinzel. — Ueber den Stil der altgermanischen Poesie. Strasburg, 1875. Opposed by

Gummere, F. B. — The Anglo-Saxon Metaphor. Freiburg-Dissertation. Halle, 1881.

Schulz, F. — Die Sprachformen des Hildebrandsliedes im Beowulf. Program of Realschule in Königsberg, 1882.

March, F. A. — The World of Beowulf. Proceedings of the Amer. Phil. Association, 1882.

Zeitschrift für deutsches Alterthum. (Haupt.)

V. 10. — Haupt, M. — Zum Beowulf.

VII. 410. — Müllenhoff, K. — Sceáf und seine Nachkommen.

VII. 524. — Bachlechner, J. — Die Merovinge im Beowulf.

XI. 59. — Bouterwek, K. W. — Zur Kritik des Beowulfliedes, 1859.

XI. 176. — Rieger, M. — Ingaevonen, Istaevonen, Herminonen.

XI. 272. — Müllenhoff, K. — Zur Kritik des A. S. Volksepos.

XI. 409. — Dietrich. — Rettungen. 1859.

XII. 259 — Müllenhoff, K. — Zeugnisse und Excurse zur deutschen Heldensage. 1865.

XIV. 193. — Müllenhoff, K. — Die innere Geschichte des Beowulfs. (1869.) Pronounces strongly in favor of separate lays.

Zeitschrift für deutsche Philologie. (Höpfner und Zacher.)

✓ II. 3u5. — Köhler, A. — Die Einleitung des Beowulfliedes, and Die beiden Episoden von Heremod. 1870.

II. 371. — Rieger, M. — Review of Heyne's 2d edition (1868).

III. 381. — Rieger, M. — Zum Beowulf. 1871.

IV. 192. — Bugge, S. — Zum Beowulf. 1873.

Germania. (Pfeiffer.)

I. 297 and 455. — Bachlechner, J. — Eomaer und Heming (Ham-lac).

I. 384. — Bouterwek. K. — Das Beowulflied. Eine Vorlesung 1856.

VIII. 489. — Holtzmann, A. — Zu Beowulf. (Textkritik.)

✓ XIII. 129. — Köhler, A. — Germanische Alterthümer im Beo-wulf.

Anglia, IV. 69. — Wülcker, R. P. — Besprechung der Beowulfüber-setzungen, im anschluss an Lumsden's translation. Full and serviceable account of the translations of " Beowulf."

Extracts from " Beowulf " may be found in

Leo's Alt- säch. u. A. S. Sprachproben. Halle, 1838.

Klipstein's Analecta Anglosaxonica. New York, 1848. Vol. II.

Ettmüller's Engla and Seaxna scôpas and bôceras. Quedlinburgii et Lipsiae, 1851. — *Ebeling's* A. S. Lesebuch. Leipzig, 1847.

Rieger's Alt- und angelsächsiches Lesebuch. Giessen, 1861.

March's Anglo-Saxon Reader. New York, 1870.

Sweet's Anglo-Saxon Reader. Oxford, 1876; 2d edition, 1879; 3d edition, 1881; 4th edition, 1884.

Literary notices and criticism of " Beowulf " may be found in the usual histories of English literature, the full-est, perhaps, in Morley's English Writers, Vol. I., Part I., London, 1867; also in his First Sketch of English Literature, London, 1873, very brief; and more fully in his Longer Works in English Verse and Prose, London, 1881, (Chap. I.). Add D'Israeli's Amenities of Liter-ature; Sweet's Introduction to Warton's History of English Poetry (Vol. II., Hazlitt's edition); Craik, a mere mention; Taine, more full; Arnold's Manual of English

Literature (English edition); Brother Azarias's ⏤evelop-
ment of English Literature: Old English Period, New
York, 1879, (reviewed by Wülcker in Anglia, IV. 3); ten
Brink's Geschichte der Englischen Literatur, I, Berlin,
1877, the best criticism, (reviewed by Wülcker in Anglia,
I. 201); Hart's Syllabus of Anglo-Saxon Literature,
adapted from ten Brink, Cincinnati, 1881; Metcalfe's
The Englishman and the Scandinavian, London, 1880,
(reviewed by Sweet in Academy, May 29, 1880); Gibb's
Gudrun and other Tales, a popular synopsis; and mere
mention in the ordinary text-book histories of English
literature, such as Spalding, Angus, Shaw (English edition corrected by American editor), Coppée, and others,
which it is scarcely worth while to enumerate, for their
notices are often so meagre as to be useless, and sometimes so incorrect that it would have been better to omit
them.

The reader may consult also the article "Beowulf" in
Chambers's Cyclopedia, published in this country in the
Library of Universal Knowledge. The latest (ninth) edi-
tion of the Encyclopædia Britannica has no such separate
title, but "Beowulf" is included in the article on English
Literature.

The above Bibliography has been compiled from various
sources, and especially from the valuable Bibliographies
annually published in connection with the above-mentioned
German philological journals, and from the book-notices
of the journals themselves.

ADDITIONS TO THE BIBLIOGRAPHY.

EDITIONS. — The completion of Wülcker's, Holder's, and Harrison and Sharp's editions of the text is noted above, and the publication of the E. E. T. Society's Facsimile of the Ms., which is to be followed by a critical text from Zupitza, with translation from Napier. The late Prof. Müllenhoff was to supply the accompanying dissertations on the composition and the mythological and historical elements, for the E. E. T. Society's edition.

TRANSLATIONS. — Lumsden's second edition is noted above; also Wülcker's second edition of Grein's translation, Cassel, 1883, reviewed by Th. Krüger in Englische Studien, VIII, 139, 1884; and the following are to be added : —

Zinsser, G. — Der Kampf Beowulfs mit Grendel. Probe einer metrischer übersetzung des A. S. epos Beowulf. Jahresbericht of the Realschule at Forbach, 1881. Reviewed in Herrig's Archiv, LXVIII, 446.

Grion, Giusto. — Beovulf, poema epico anglo-sassone del VII secolo, tradotto e illustrato. Lucca, 1883. Dagli Atti dell' Accademia Lucchese, Vol. XXII. The first Italian translation.

GENERAL WORKS, DISSERTATIONS, ETC., in which discussions of "Beowulf," or references to it, may be found are : —

Outzen. — Ueber das A. S. Beowulfs Gedicht. Kieler Blätter, III, 312, 1816.

Kemble, J. M., and Wright, T., in the Gentleman's Magazine for 1834 and 1835, a controversy.

De Larenaudière, P., and Michel, F. — Anglo-Saxonica, I and II, 1836 and 1837; the former a translation of Wright's Anglo-Saxon Language and Poetry, with criticism of "Beowulf," and the latter containing Kemble's textual criticisms of

Grimm and Conybeare, prefixed to Michel's Bibliotheca
Anglo-Saxonica, *q.v.*

Rask, E. — Grammar of the Anglo-Saxon Tongue, translated by
B. Thorpe, 1830. New edition, 1879.

Taylor, W. — Historic Survey of German Poetry, 3 vols., 1830.

Guest, E. — History of English Rhythms, 2 vols., 1838. Edited
by W. W. Skeat in 1 vol., 1882. Reviewed by J. M. Garnett
in Am. Jour. of Philology, IV, 478, 1883. (Cf. also my review
of Schipper's Englische Metrik, I, in Am. Jour. of Philology,
III, 355, 1882.)

[*Longfellow, H. W.*] — Anglo-Saxon Literature. N. Am. Review,
XLVII, No. 100, for July, 1838; and his Poets and Poetry of
Europe. New edition, 1871.

Petheram, J. — Historical Sketch of Anglo-Saxon Literature in
England, 1840.

Wright, T. — Biographia Britannica Literaria, Vol. I, Anglo-
Saxon Period, 1842 ; his Celt, Roman, and Saxon, 1852; 2d ·
edition, 1875; and his Essays on the Literature, etc., of the
Middle Ages, 2 vols., 1846.

Lappenberg, J. M. — History of England under the Anglo-Saxon
Kings. Translated by B. Thorpe, 2 vols., 1845.

—— Heimskringla. Edinburgh Review, LXXXII, No. 166, for
Oct., 1845. Contains brief notice of Anglo-Saxon poetry.

Kemble, J. M. — Saxons in England, 2 vols., 1849.

Green, J. R. — The Making of England, 1882.

Grundtvig, N. F. S. — Norden's Mythologi, 1808 ; 2d edition,
1832; 3d edition, 1869; and his Dannewirke, 1817, II, 284,
containing identification of Chocilaicus with Hygelac. (Cf.
Krüger, in Englische Studien, VIII, 137, with Thorpe's Introduction, p. xxvi, note.)

Grimm, J. — Deutsche Mythologie, 1835; 2d edition, 1844; 3d
edition, 1854; 4th edition, by E. H. Meyer, 3 vols., 1875, translated by J. S. Stallybrass, London, 1880, *sqq.;* also his Kleinere
Schriften, II, 211, and IV, 178, 5 vols., 1864–70; and his
Geschichte der Deutschen Sprache, 4th edition, 1880.

Mone, F. J. — Untersuchungen zur Geschichte der teutschen
Heldensage, 1836.

Grimm, W. — Die Deutsche Heldensage. 2d edition, by K. Müllenhoff, 1867.

Simrock, K. — Handbuch der Deutschen Mythologie, 1878.

Wagner, W. — Deutsche Heldensage, 1881; and

Wagner, W., and *McDowall, M. W.* — Epics and Romances of the Middle Ages, 1883.

↖ *Weinhold.* — Altnordisches Leben, 1856.

Ettmüller, L. — Handbuch der Deutschen Literaturgeschichte, 1847.

Earle, J. — Anglo-Saxon Literature, 1884. Reviewed in The Nation, No. 1002, Sept. 11, 1884.

Müllenhoff, K. — Die Austrasische Dietrichssage, Haupt's Zeitschrift, VI, 437, 1848 ; and Der Mythus von Beowulf, VII, 419, 1849.

Lichtenheld, A. — Das schwache Adjectiv im Angelsächsischen, Haupt's Zeitschrift, XVI, 325, 1873.

Arndt, O. — Ueber die altgermanische epische Sprache. Paderborn, 1877.

Bernhardt, E. — Zur Gotischen Casuslehre, II. Zeitschrift für Deutsche Philologie, XIII, 1, 1881.

Nader, E. — Der Genetiv im Beowulf. Program of the Staatsoberrealschule in Brünn, 1882 ; reviewed by Klinghardt in Englische Studien, VI, 288, 1883 ; and Dativ und Instrumental im Beowulf. Jahresbericht of the Vienna communal Oberrealschule, 1882–83 ; reviewed by Klinghardt in Englische Studien, VII, 368, 1884.

Hotz, G. — On the Use of the Subjunctive Mood in Anglo-Saxon, and its further history in Old English. Zürich, 1882. Reviewed by Wissmann in Literaturblatt für germ. und rom. Philologie, IV, 2, February, 1883.

Schemann, K. — Die Synonyma im Beowulfsliede, mit Rücksicht auf Composition und Poetik des Gedichts. Hagen, 1882. Reviewed by Kluge in Literaturblatt, IV, 2, February, 1883.

Schemann, K. — Beowulf. Antichissimo poema epico de' popoli Germanici. Giornale Neapolitano di filosofia e lettere, scienze morale e politiche, IV, Vol. VII, 63, 175.

↙ *Hoffmann, A.* — Der bildliche Ausdruck im Beowulf und in der Edda. Englische Studien, VI, 163, 1883.

Möller, H. — Das altenglische Volksepos in der ursprünglichen strophischen Form. I, Abhandlungen. II, Texte. Kiel, 1883. Reviewed by Heinzel in Zeitschrift für deutsches Alterthum, XXVIII (XVI), 215, 1884.

Rönning, F. — Beovulfs-Kvadet. En literaer-historisk undersögelse. Copenhagen, 1883. Reviewed by Heinzel in Z. für d. Alterthum, XXVIII (XVI), 233, 1884.

Kluge, F. — Sprachhistorische Miscellen. Paul und Braune, Beiträge, VIII, 532, 1882; and Zum Beowulf, IX, 187, 1883.

Cosijn, P. J. — Zum Beowulf. Paul und Braune, VIII, 508, 1882.

Sievers, E. — Zum Beowulf. Paul und Braune, IX, 135 and 370, 1883.

Merbot, R. — Aesthetische Studien zur angelsächsichen Poesie. Breslau, 1883. Cf. Anglia, VI, Anzeiger, 100.

Krüger, Th. — Ueber Ursprung und Entwickelung des Beowulf-liedes. Herrig's Archiv, LXXI, 129, 1884; and Zum Beowulf-liede. Program des städtischen Realgymnasiums in Bromberg, 1884. Both useful summaries of the literature and present state of "Beowulf" criticism. The latter contains also re-marks on the metre.

Reviews of the first edition of this translation which deserve mention here will be found in The Nation, No. 919, Feb. 8, 1883; the American Journal of Philology, IV, 84, by J. A. H., with which compare my letter, IV, 242, 1883; Literaturblatt für germanische und romanische Philologie, IV, No. 10, Oct., 1883, by James W. Bright; Anglia, Anzeiger VI, 120, 1884, by J. Schipper; and Englische Studien, VIII, 133, 1884, by Th. Krüger, the fullest criticism.

Each year adds to "Beowulf" literature in Germany; Denmark, Holland, France, and now Italy, have shown their appreciation of this great poem; England and America have supplied texts and translations, but have been content to leave criticism to Germany, for, since Kemble, no thorough criticism of this ancestral heirloom has proceeded from an Englishman or an American.

Further Additions to the Bibliography.

Editions.

Harrison, J. A., and *Sharp, R.* — Beowulf, 2d ed., revised, Boston, 1885 ; 3d ed., corrected and enlarged, 1888 ; 4th ed., revised, with notes, 1894.

Socin, A. — Heyne's Beowulf, 5th ed., Paderborn and Münster, 1888. Rev. by E. Sievers in Z. für d. Philologie, XXI, 354–365 ; and by R. Heinzel in Z. für d. Alterthum, XXIII, Anzeiger, XV, 189–194.

Translations.

Wickberg, R. — Beowulf, en fornengelek hjeltedikt, öfersatt. Westervik. The first Swedish translation.

Essays, Dissertations, and Histories of Literature.

Earle, J. — Beowulf. Canadian Monthly, II, 83, 1872.

——— — Beowulf. Household Words, XVII, 459.

——— — Beowulf. London Times, Weekly ed., Oct. 9, 1885.

Gibb, John. — Gudrun, Beowulf, and Roland, 2d ed., London, 1883. Rev. in Revue Critique, No. 49, 1883.

Powell, F. York-. — Recent Beowulf Literature (Harrison, Holder, Lumsden). Academy, No. 648, Oct. 4, 1884.

——— — Harrison's "Beowulf." Academy, No. 654, Nov. 15, 1884.

Harrison, J. A. — Beowulf. Academy, No. 653, Nov. 8, 1884.

——— — List of Irregular (Strong) Verbs in "Beowulf." Amer. Journal of Philology, IV, 462, 1883.

——— — Old Teutonic Life in "Beowulf." Overland Monthly, July, 1884, 1–21.

Bright, J. W. — Review of Harrison and Sharp's "Beowulf," 1st ed. Litteraturblatt für germ. und rom. Philologie, June, 1884.

Skeat, W. W. — The Monster Grendel in "Beowulf," with a Discussion of Lines 2076–2100. Journal of Philology, No. 29, XV, 120–131.

xxxviii

Gummere, F. B. — The Translation of "Beowulf." Amer. Journal of Philology, VII, 46–78, 1886.

Tolman, A. H. — The Style of Anglo-Saxon Poetry. Transactions of the Modern Language Association of America, Vol. III, 1887.

Schilling, H. — The Finnsburg-Fragment and the Finn-Episode. Mod. Lang. Notes, II, 291, June, 1887.

Corson, H. — A Passage of Beowulf [2724 ff.]. Mod. Lang. Notes, III, 193, April, 1888.

Davidson, Chas. — Differences between the Scribes of "Beowulf." Mod. Lang. Notes, V, 85 and 378, Febr. and June, 1890.

McClumpha, Chas. F. — Differences between the Scribes of "Beowulf." Mod. Lang. Notes, V, 245, April, 1890.

Fahlbeck, P. — Beovulfsqvädet, Såsom källa för nordisk fornhistoria. Antiquarisk Tidskrift för Sverige, VIII, 1–87, 1884(?). Rev. in The Academy, No. 713.

Hertz, W. — Beowulf, das älteste germanische Epos. Nord und Süd, XXIX, 229–253, May, 1884.

Hirt, H. — Untersuchungen zur west-germanischen verskunst. Heft I. Kritik der neuern theorien. Metrik der A.-S. Leipzig, 1889.

Lehmann, H. — Brünne und helm im angelsächsischen Beowulfliede. Leipzig, 1885. Rev. by R. Wülker in Anglia, VIII, Anzeiger, 167; and by A. Schulz in Englische Studien, IX, 471.

—— — Ueber die waffen im angelsächsischen Beowulfliede. Germania, XXXI (XIX), 486–497.

Banning, A. — Die epischen Formeln im Beowulf. I. Die verbalen Synonyma. Doctor-dissertation. Marburg, 1886.

Bode, W. — Die Kenningar in der angelsächsischen Dichtung. Strassburger dissertation. Darmstadt and Leipzig, 1886.

Köhler, K. — Der syntaktische Gebrauch des Infinitivs und Particips im Beowulf. Doctor-dissertation. Münster, 1886.

Schneider, F. — Der Kampf mit Grendels Mutter. Program des Friedrichs-Realgymnasiums. Berlin, 1887.

Krüger, Th. — Zum Beowulf. Paul and Braune's Beiträge, IX, 571–5.8.

Sievers, E. — Zur rhythmik des germ. alliterationsverses. I. Vorbemerkungen. Die metrik des Beowulf. P. & B., X, 209–314. II. Sprachliche ergebnisse. P. & B., X, 451–545.

—— — Die heimat des Beowulf-dichters. P. & B., XI, 354–362.

—— — Altnordisches im Beowulf? P. & B., XII, 168–200.

—— — Der angelsächsische Schwellvers. P. & B., XII, 454–482.

Sarrazin, G. — Der schauplatz des ersten Beowulfliedes und die heimat des dichters. P. & B., XI, 159–183.

——— — Altnordisches im Beowulfliede. P. &. B., XI, 528–541.

——— — Die Beowulfsage in Dänemark. Anglia, IX, 195–199, 1886.

——— — Beowa und Böthvar. Anglia, IX, 200-204.

——— — Beowulf und Kynewulf. Anglia, IX, 515–550.

——— — Beowulf-Studien. Berlin, 1888. Rev. by E. Sievers in Z. für d. Philologie, XXI, 366; by R. Heinzel in Z. für d. Alterthum, XXIII, Anzeiger, XV, 182–189; by R. Wülker in Anglia, XI, 536–539; and by F. Dieter in Herrig's Archiv, 83, 352.

Bugge, S. — Studien über das Beowulfepos. P. & B., XII, 1–80, and 360–375.

Kittredge, G. — Zu Beowulf, 107 ff. P. & B., XIII, 210,

ten Brink, B. — Beowulf. Untersuchungen. Quellen und Forschungen, 62. Strassburg and London, 1888. Rev. by R. Heinzel in Z. für d. Alterthum, XXIII, Anzeiger, XV, 153–182; by E. Koeppel in Z. für d. Philologie, XXI, 113–122; by H. Möller in Englische Studien, XIII, 247–315; and by R. Wülker in Anglia, XI, 319–321.

Müllenhoff, K. — Beowulf. Untersuchungen. Berlin, 1889. Rev. by R. Heinzel in Z. für d. Alterthum, XXIII, 264–275; and by E. Koeppel in Z. für d. Philologie, XXI, 110–113.

Other reviews of Sarrazin's, ten Brink's, and Müllenhoff's works will be found noted in the *Jahresbericht für die Erscheinungen auf dem Gebiete der germanischen Philologie* for 1888, 1889, and 1890.

Nader, E. — Tempus und Modus im Beowulf. Anglia, X, 542–563, 1888, and XI, 444–499, 1889.

Miller, Thos. — The Position of Grendel's Arm in Heorot. Anglia, XII, 396–400, 1889.

Zupitza, J. — Zu Beowulf, 850. Herrig's Archiv, 84, 124, 1890.

Kennedy, H. M. — Translation of ten Brink's "Early English Literature." New York, 1883. German edition noted before.

Robinson, W. Clarke. — Introduction to our Early English Literature. London, Durham, and Heidelberg, 1885.

Engel, E. — Geschichte der englischen Litteratur. Leipzig, 1883.

Wülker, R. — Grundriss zur Geschichte der angelsächsischen Litteratur. Leipzig, 1885. An indispensable work. English translation, with additions, in preparation.

Ebert, A. — Allgemeine Geschichte der Litteratur des Mittelalters im Abendlande, Vol. III. Leipzig, 1887.

Morley, H. — English Writers. New ed., Vol. I. London, 1887. Cf. my review in Mod. Lang. Notes, III, 380, June, 1888.

Deskau, H. — Zum Studium des Beowulf. Berichte des freien deutschen Hochstiftes, 1890.

Joseph, E. — Zwei Versversetzungen im Beowulf. Z. für d. Philologie, XXII, 385-397.

Klöpper, C. — Heorot-Hall in the Anglo-Saxon Poem of "Beowulf." Festschrift für K. E. Krause. Rostock.

Sarrazin, G. — Entgegnung. Englische Studien, XIV, 421-427, a reply to E. Koeppel's review of Sarrazin's Beowulf-Studien, Eng. Stud., XIII, 475. Cf. Koeppel's answer, Eng. Stud., XIV, 427-432.

Schröer, A. — Zur Texterklärung des Beowulf. Anglia, XIII, 333-348, 1890.

Sievers, E. — Zur Texterklärung des Beowulf. Anglia, XIV, 133-146, 1891.

Garnett, J. M. — The Translation of Anglo-Saxon Poetry. Publications of the Modern Language Association of America, Vol. VI, No. 3, 1891.

Davidson, Chas. — The Phonology of the Stressed Vowels in "Béowulf." Publications of the Modern Language Association of America, Vol. VI, No. 3, 1891.

Erdmann, A. — Ueber die Heimat und den Namen der Angeln. Upsala, 1890-91.

Horning, E. L. — Zur Grammatik des Beowulf. Göttingen Doctor-Dissertation, 1891.

Cosijn, P. J. — Aanteekeningen op den Beowulf. Leiden, 1892.

Earle, J. — The Deeds of Beowulf. A prose translation, with introduction and notes. Oxford, 1892.

Hall, J. L. — Beowulf, translated from the Heym-Socin text. Boston, 1892. Rev. by O. Glöde, Englische Studien, XIX, 257.

Sarrazin, G. — Die Abfassungszeit des Beowulfliedes. I. Anglia, XIV, 399-415, 1892.

Brooke, S. A. — The History of Early English Literature, Chs. II-V. New York and London, 1892.

Hoffmann, P. — Beowulf. Aeltestes deutsches Heldengedicht. Aus dem Angelsächsischen übertragen. Züllichau, 1893. Rev. by O. Glöde, Englische Studien, XIX, 412.

Todt, A. — Die Wortstellung im Beowulf. Anglia, XVI, 226-260, 1893.

Wyatt, A. J. — Beowulf. Edited with textual foot-notes, etc. Cambridge, 1894. Rev. by H. Bradley, Academy, No. 1160, July 28, 1894.

The Fight at Finnsburg.

THIS fragment was discovered by Hickes, bound with a manuscript of Homilies, in the archiepiscopal library of Lambeth, and was first published by him in his Thesaurus linguarum veterum septentrionalium, I, 192. It has been since published by Conybeare in his Illustrations of Anglo-Saxon Poetry, Ettmüller in his *Scôpas and Bôceras*, and by Kemble, Schaldemose, Thorpe, Grundtvig, Grein, and Heyne in their editions of "Beowulf." From its contents it relates evidently to the episode of Finn, occurring in "Beowulf," 1068–1159, but there is no reason to think that it ever formed a part of that poem. It contains some fuller particulars of that noted fight, and introduces personages not mentioned in "Beowulf." It represents Hnaef the Dane and his sixty warriors defending themselves in a building against the attack of Finn, and so connects itself with the first part of the episode of Finn, before the fall of Hnaef and the leadership of Hengest. Heyne's Glossary omits the words and proper names peculiar to this poem, and it is not translated by either Grein or Heyne. The leaf on which it was written is lost, so that the text depends on Hickes's publication. The text is given also in Klipstein's Analecta Anglo-Saxonica, Vol. II, p. 426; Rieger's Lesebuch; Wülcker's Kleinere A. S. Dichtungen (1882), and his edition of Grein's *Bibliothek*, Vol. I. A criticism of the text by Grein is in Germania, X; a Latin translation in Conybeare; English, in Conybeare, Thorpe, and Haigh; Danish, in Grundtvig's and Schaldemose's, and German, in Ettmüller's and Simrock's translations of "Beowulf."

GLOSSARY OF PROPER NAMES.

Aelfhere. — A kinsman of Wiglaf.

Aeschere. — A counsellor of Hrothgar, elder brother of Yrmen-laf. Slain by Grendel's mother.

Beanstan. — Father of Breca.

Beowulf (1). — A Dane. Son of Scyld, and father of Healf-dene.

Beowulf (2). — A Geat. Hero of the poem. Son of Ecgtheow and a daughter of Hrethel, king of the Geats, at whose court he was brought up. Though indolent in his youth, when a man he has the strength of thirty men, and is noted for his prowess. Has a swimming-match with Breca in his youth. Goes with fourteen Geats to help Hrothgar against Grendel, whom he conquers, and is rewarded by Hrothgar. Overcomes Grendel's mother and returns home. After Hygelac's death in battle with the Franks, Frisians, and Hugs, from which Beowulf escapes after killing Daeghrefn, the Hug, he acts as regent for Heardred, Hygelac's son, and after his death Beowulf succeeds to the throne. He kills Eadgils the Scylfing in revenge for the murder of Heardred, and probably subdues his land. Fights with the dragon, and kills him, but receives a mortal wound. His death and burial end the poem.

Breca. — Son of Beanstan. Prince of the Brondings. Has a swimming-match with Beowulf.

Brondings. — A tribe whose ruler is Breca.

Brosinga mene. — A noted necklace, or collar, which the Bro-sings once possessed. (See Arnold's *Excursus*.)

Cain. — Grendel's race are his descendants.

Daeghrefn. — A warrior of the Hugs, who seems to have been the murderer of Hygelac. Was killed by Beowulf.

Danes. — As subjects of Scyld and his descendants, called also Scyldings, and after Ing, first king of the East-Danes, Ing-wine; also once, Hrethmen. From their shining armor called *Gâr-* (Spear-) Danes, *Hring-* (Ring-) Danes, and *Beorht-* (Bright-) Danes; known also as North-, South-, East-, and West-Danes. They dwell in Scedelands, Scedenig, by two seas, *i.e.*, Zealand and southern coast of Sweden.

Ecglaf. — Father of Hunferth.

Ecgtheow. — Father of Beowulf the Geat, of the family of the Waegmundings. Slew Heatholaf among the Wylfings, and hence crosses the sea to the Danes, whose king, Hrothgar, settles the quarrel with a money-payment.

Ecgwela. — The Scyldings are called his descendants. Grein considers him the founder of the older dynasty of Danish kings, which ended with Heremod.

Elan. — Daughter of Healfdene, and supposed to be the wife of Ongentheow, the Scylfing.

Earna naes. — The *Eagles' ness* in the land of the Geats, at which Beowulf's fight with the dragon took place.

Eadgils. — Son of Ohthere, and grandson of Ongentheow.

Eaha. — A Dane, companion of Hnaef and Hengest. Finnsburg, l. 15.

Eanmund. — Brother of Eadgils. What is stated about these two sons of Ohthere is not altogether clear, and is differently interpreted by editors, according as *freónd* (friend) or *feónd* (enemy) is read in line 2393. Heyne reads *feónd*, and says that Eanmund and Eadgils rebelled against their father, and were driven from the Sweons' kingdom (Sweden). They went to Heardred, probably with hostile intent. At all events Heardred was slain at a feast by one of them, presumably Eanmund, for Weohstan slays him in revenge for his murdered king, and takes the arms presented to Eanmund by his uncle Onela. After the death of Heardred and Eanmund, Eadgils returns to his home, his father, Ohthere, having died meanwhile, but must yield to Beowulf, who has ascended the throne. He makes an inroad later into the land of the Geats, and is killed by Beowulf, who assumes the rule over the Sweons, if we read *Scylfingas*, 3005, which alone seems to give good sense, for Ms. *Scyldingas*. Grein reads *freónd*, 2393, and understands that Eadgils returns to his country, supported by Beowulf, with an army, kills his uncle, Onela, and probably becomes himself king of the Sweons. Heyne's view seems more consistent with the preceding statements, but is inadmissible, as it is contrary to the Ms. reading in 2393.

Eofor. — A Geat. Son of Wonred, and brother of Wulf. Kills Ongentheow, and Hygelac gives him his only daughter in marriage, and other gifts.

Eormenric. — King of the Goths. Hama stole from him the *Brosinga mene.*

Eomaer. — Son of Offa and Thrytho.

Finn. — Son of Folcwalda, king of the North-Frisians and Jutes, and husband of Hildeburg, daughter of Hoce. He is the hero of the song on the Fight at Finnsburg, which is closely connected with the minstrel's song in " Beowulf," ll. 1068 *et seqq.* Heyne explains the sequence of events as follows : Hnaef, a Dane, and probably brother of Hildeburg, is, with his following of sixty men, a guest of Finn at his city, Finnsburg in Jutland. The Danes are treacherously attacked at night by Finn's men. They hold the doors of their besieged dwelling for five days without losing a man : then Hnaef is slain, and Hengest takes command of the ·Danes. But Finn's band has suffered severely : Hildeburg mourns for a son and a brother. The Frisians offer the Danes peace on certain conditions, which are sworn to, and Finn makes restitution by a money-payment. Now, according to Grein, all who have survived the fight go together to Friesland, Finn's proper residence, and Hengest stays through the winter, detained by ice and storms. But in the spring the feud breaks out afresh. Guthlaf and Oslaf, who have probably been sent for as aid, avenge Hnaef's death, the hall is filled with the corpses of their foes, Finn himself is slain, his queen taken prisoner, and, with the plundered treasures, is carried to the Danes' land. (See also Arnold's *Excursus.*)

Finna land. — The land of the Finns. Beowulf reaches it in his swimming-match with Breca.

Finnsburg. — The city of Finn, probably in Jutland.

Fitela. — Son of the Waelsing Sigemund and his sister Signy, and Sigemund's companion in fight. The Sinfiötli of the Völsunga Saga. (See William Morris's *Sigurd the Volsung,* Book I.)

Folcwalda. — Father of Finn.

Franks. — King Hygelac is killed in an expedition against the Franks, Frisians, and Hugs.

Frisians. — Divided into North-Frisians, whose king is Finn, and West-Frisians, in alliance with the Franks and Hugs.

Freswael. — The battle-place in North-Friesland where Hnaef fell, according to Grein; but the Ms. reading is *Fr . . es wæl,* so Heyne defines it simply as an illegible proper name.

Freaware. — Daughter of Hrothgar, married to Ingeld, son of Froda, king of the Heathobards, to appease a quarrel between the Danes and the Heathobards.

Froda. — Father of Ingeld, and king of the Heathobards.

Garmund. — Father of Offa, and grandfather of Eomaer.

Garulf. — One of Finn's men. Finnsburg, ll. 18, 31.

Geats. — A people in southern Scandinavia. Called also *Weder-* (Weather-) Geats or Weders, *Gûð-* (War-) Geats, and *Sæ-* (Sea-) Geats. Their kings are Hrethel, his sons Haethcyn and Hygelac, his son Heardred, and then Beowulf, hero of the poem.

Gifths. — Probably Gepidae, mentioned along with the Spear-Danes and Sweons, or Swedes.

Grendel. — A demon of the fens, of Cain's race. He breaks into Hrothgar's hall at night and carries off thirty men. This goes on for twelve years, until Beowulf fights with him, and inflicts a deadly wound by tearing out his arm, which is placed on the roof of Heorot as a sign of victory. Grendel's mother, to avenge her son, breaks into the hall the following night and carries off Aeschere. Beowulf seeks her dwelling-place in the mere, fights with her, and kills her, cuts off the head of Grendel, and brings it to Hrothgar.

Guthhere. — One of Finn's men. Finnsburg, l. 20.

Guthlaf (1). — A Dane, with Hnaef and Hengest. Finnsburg, l. 18.

     (2). — A Frisian, father of Garulf. Finnsburg, l. 35.

Halga. — Younger brother of Hrothgar, and father of Hrothulf.

Hama. — Stole the *Brosinga mene* from Eormenric.

Haereth. — Father of Hygd, wife of Hygelac.

Haethcyn. — Second son of Hrethel. Accidentally kills his eldest brother Herebeald with an arrow. Succeeds to the kingdom after Hrethel's death, and falls in battle at the Ravens' wood against the Swedish king Ongentheow.

Helmings. — Family to which Wealhtheow, Hrothgar's wife, belongs.

Heming. — Offa and Eomaer are called Heming's kinsmen. According to Bachlechner (*Germania I*, 458), Heming is a sister's son of Garmund, father of Offa.

Hengest. — A Dane, who takes command after Hnaef's death. Finnsburg, l. 19. (See Finn.)

Herebeald. — Eldest son of Hrethel, accidentally killed with an arrow by his brother Haethcyn.

Heremod. — King of the Danes, not belonging to the dynasty of the Scyldings, but, according to Grein, perhaps to the one immediately preceding. Was banished on account of his unheard-of cruelty.

Hereric. — Uncle of Heardred, otherwise unknown.

Hetwars. — Franks, which see. Probably Chatti or Chatuarii.

Healfdene. — Son of Beowulf the Scylding, and king of the Danes, whom he long rules. Has three sons, Heorogar, Hrothgar, and Halga, and a daughter, Elan.

Heardred. — Son of Hygelac and Hygd. Though still a minor, succeeds his father, and Beowulf, his father's nephew, acts as regent until he is of age. Is slain by the sons of Ohthere, which murder Beowulf avenges afterwards on Eadgils.

Heathobards. — The tribe of Lombards. Their king Froda fell in war with the Danes. To appease the feud Hrothgar marries his daughter Freaware to Froda's son Ingeld, but this does not succeed, for Ingeld afterwards avenges his father's death on the Danes.

Heatholaf. — A warrior of the Wylfings, slain by Ecgtheow, Beowulf's father.

Heathoremes. — Breca reaches their land in the swimming-match with Beowulf.

Heorogar. — Son of Healfdene, and father of Heoroweard. Beowulf receives his cuirass from Hrothgar, and presents it to Hygelac.

Heoroweard. — Son of Heorogar.

Heorot. — Hrothgar's great hall, built with extraordinary magnificence. Beowulf's fight with Grendel takes place in it. It takes its name from the stag's antlers which adorn the eastern and western gables.

Hildeburg. — Daughter of Hoce, kinswoman of Hnaef, wife of Finn, after whose fall she is led into captivity by the Danes.

Hnaef. — A Hocing, chieftain of Healfdene. (See Finn.)

Hondsclo. — A warrior of the Geats, killed by Grendel.

Hoce. — Father of Hildeburg, and probably of Hnaef.

Hrethel. — King of the Geats, son of Swerting. His daughter
is married to Ecgtheow, and his sons are Herebeald, Haethcyn, and Hygelac. He grieves to death on account of the
accidental shooting of Herebeald by Haethcyn.

Hrethla. — Same as Hrethel; former possessor of Beowulf's
cuirass.

Hrethmen. — The Danes.

Hrethric. — Son of Hrothgar and Wealhtheow.

Hreosna-beorh (-mount). — Promontory in the land of the
Geats, where Onela and Ohthere made inroads into the
land after Hrethel's death, which was the cause of the war
in which Haethcyn fell.

Hrothgar. — Of the dynasty of the Scyldings. Second of the
three sons of Healfdene, and king of the Danes. His wife
is Wealhtheow, his sons Hrethric and Hrothmund, and his
daughter Freaware, married to Ingeld. His great hall,
Heorot, is nightly visited by Grendel, who, with his mother,
is killed by Beowulf, for which Hrothgar gives Beowulf
costly presents. He is praised as liberal, brave, and wise.
Other events of his reign are merely alluded to.

Hrothmund. — Son of Hrothgar and Wealhtheow.

Hrothulf. — Probably a son of Halga. Wealhtheow expresses
the hope that, in case of Hrothgar's death, he will be a good
guardian to her son, which hope does not seem to be ful-
filled, for Hrothulf did not keep faith with Hrothgar.

Hrunting. — Name of Hunferth's sword.

Hugs. — Tribe united with Franks and Frisians. Probably the
Chauci.

Hunferth. — Son of Ecglaf, and orator of Hrothgar. Killed his
brothers. Lent his sword Hrunting to Beowulf in the fight
with Grendel's mother.

Hunlafing. — According to Heyne, name of a costly sword which
Finn gives to Hengest. According to Grein, name of one
of Finn's warriors, who slays Hengest. Heyne's view
seems the most probable.

Hygd. — Daughter of Haereth and wife of Hygelac. Her noble
character is praised in the episode of Thrytho.

Hygelac. — King of the Geats. Son of Hrethel, grandson of
Swerting, and uncle of Beowulf. Comes to the throne
after his brother Haethcyn is killed by Ongentheow. Gives
his only daughter in marriage to Eofor as reward for kill-

ing Ongentheow. We afterwards find him married to the young Hygd, so that she seems to be his second wife. Heardred is their son. Falls in an expedition against the Franks, Frisians, and Hugs.

Ingeld. — Son of Froda, prince of the Heathobards, who falls in a fight with the Danes, and, to appease the quarrel, Hrothgar marries his daughter Freaware to Ingeld, but, urged by an old warrior, he afterwards takes revenge for the death of his father.

Ingwine. — Friends of Ing, first king of the East-Danes, hence used as a name for the Danes.

Jutes (*Eotenas*). — A people of Jutland, over whom the Frisian king Finn rules.*

Merwings. — Name of the Franks, still ruled by the Merovingian kings.

Modthrytho. — See Thrytho.

Naegling. — Name of Beowulf's sword.

Offa. — King of the Angles. Son of Garmund. Married to Thrytho, a beautiful but cruel woman.

Ohthere. — Son of Ongentheow, and father of Eanmund and Eadgils.

Onela. — Brother of Ohthere.

Ongentheow. — King of the Sweons, or Swedes, of the dynasty of the Scylfings. His wife is perhaps Elan, daughter of Healfdene. She (or a second wife) is taken prisoner by Haethcyn on a raid into Sweden, and released by Ongentheow, who kills Haethcyn, and besieges the Geats in Raven's wood, from which siege they are delivered by Hygelac. In the battle which ensues Ongentheow is attacked by the brothers Wulf and Eofor, and slain by the latter.

Ordlaf. — A warrior of Hnaef and Hengest, who holds the doors with Guthlaf. Finnsburg, l. 18.

Oslaf. — A warrior of Hengest, who revenges his death on Finn.

Scedeland, Scedenig. — The southern portion of the Scandinavian peninsula, belonging to the Danes, and used to denote the Danish kingdom in general.

Scef. — Father of Scyld.

* In his 4th ed. Heyne no longer takes *Eotenas* as a proper name, but same as *eoton* = giant, and explains it as a hurtful foe, used sometimes of the Danes, and sometimes of the Frisians.

Scyld. — Father of Beowulf the Dane, and grandfather of Healf-dene. At his death his body is committed to an ornamented vessel and given to the sea, just as he, when a child, had been brought to the Danes' land.

Scyldings. — Name of the Danes, and of the dynasty by which they are ruled. The Danes are called also *Âr-* (Honor-) Scyldings, *Sige-* (Victory-) Scyldings, *Theôd-* (Folk-) Scyldings, and *Here-* (Army-) Scyldings.

Scylfings. — A Swedish royal family, whose relationships extend to the Geats also, as Wiglaf, son of Weohstan, and kinsman of Beowulf, is called a Waegmunding and a prince of the Scylfings. The Scylfings are called also *Heaðo-* (Battle-) Scylfings and *Gûð-* (War-) Scylfings.

Secgs. — Name of a tribe to which Sigeferth belongs. Finnsburg, l. 26.

Sigeferth. — A warrior of Hnaef and Hengest, who holds the doors with Eaha. Finnsburg, l. 17.

Sigemund. — Son of Waels. Fitela is his son and nephew. Fights with the dragon, kills him, and robs the hoard. (See William Morris's *Sigurd the Volsung*, Book I.)

Swerting. — Grandfather of Hygelac.

Sweons. — The Swedes, ruled over by the Scylfings.

Thrytho. — Wife of Offa, king of the Angles, and mother of Eomaer, known for her fierce and cruel disposition, so forming a contrast to the gentle and lovable Hygd. This Offa lived about the middle of the 4th century. (See Heyne's note to 1927, Suchier in Paul and Braune's *Beitraege*, IV. 500, and Grein in Ebert's *Jahrbuch*, IV. 279, who, however, takes the name to be Modthrytho, but Thrytho, as given by Heyne and others, suits better.)

Waegmundings. — This family includes Weohstan and his son Wiglaf, Ecgtheow and his son Beowulf. They are a branch of the Scylfings.

Waels. — Father of Sigemund.

Waras. — Name of a people mentioned in l. 461, for which Heyne reads Weders.

Wealhtheow. — Wife of Hrothgar, of the race of the Helmings and mother of Hrethric, Hrothmund, and Freaware.

Weders. — Name of the Geats.

Weland. — The noted smith, maker of Beowulf's cuirass.

Wendlas. — A tribe whose chief is Wulfgar. According to Grundtvig and Bugge, they dwelt in Wendill, the most northern district of Jutland. Probably Vandals.

Weohstan. — A Waegmunding. Father of Wiglaf. He is the slayer of Eanmund, in revenge for his murdered king Heardred.

Wiglaf. — Son of Weohstan, kinsman of Aelfhere. Helps Beowulf in his fight with the dragon, and receives from him his ring, helmet, and cuirass.

Withergyld. — Name of a Heathobard warrior, killed by the Danes, according to Grein, but Heyne does not take the word as a proper name, l. 2051.

Wonred. — Father of Wulf and Eofor.

Wulf. — A Geat. Son of Wonred. Fights in battle with Ongentheow, and wounds him, but is himself severely wounded, whereupon Eofor slays Ongentheow.

Wulfgar. — Chief of the Wendlas. Lives at Hrothgar's court, and is his messenger and servant.

Wylfings. — A tribe, whose warrior Heatholaf is slain by Ecgtheow.

Yrmenlaf. — Brother of Aeschere.

LIST OF OLD-ENGLISH WORDS.

Aetheling. — (A. S. æðeling, G. Edeling.) One of noble descent. Used of those of royal family, and of the noble-born in general.

Bale. — (A. S. bealu.) Used of evil generally, especially in composition, as life-bale, night-bale, &c.

Bill. — (A. S. bil, G. Bil.) Sword. So used in Beowulf, though Grein gives also "battle-axe." Seen in composition, as battle-bill, war-bill.

Brand. — (O. N. brand-r.) Sword; in composition, battle-brand; but A. S. brand = "fire," and so used by Heyne in 1454, where Grein reads brondne, as adj., = "flaming."

Burnie. — (A. S. byrne, G. Brünne.) Coat-of-mail, corslet, cuirass. Made of chain-rings, hence ringed burnie. In composition, war-burnie, &c.

Eoten. — (A. S. *eoton.*) Giant. Acc. to Heyne, used of foes in general, and so applied to the Danes and Frisians in passages where Grein reads as proper name, = *Jutes*, e.g., 1073, 1089, 1142, 1146. In composition, eoten-race, eoten-guard.

Holm. — (A. S. *holm*, G. Holm.) Sea, sea-waves. Not islet, as in modern English. In composition, holm-cliff.

Mere. — (A. S. *mere*, G. Meer.) Sea, lake. In composition, mere-beast, &c.

Ness. — (A. S. *næs.*) Cliff, headland, promontory. In composition, sea-ness.

Nicker. — (A. S. *nicor*, G. Nix.) Sea-monster, water-spirit. Used of the sea-beasts that Beowulf kills.

Sark. — (A. S. *serce, syrce.*) Coat-of-mail, cuirass, armor. In composition, body-sark, war-sark, &c.

Scope. — (A. S. *scop.*) Minstrel, singer, poet. The invariable attendant of the feasts.

Sty. — (A. S. *stigan*, G. steigen.) To ascend, mount, and to go, in general. Frequent in Early English.

Weeds. — (A. S. *ge-wǽde.*) Clothing, especially armor, as in composition, battle-weeds, war-weeds.

Weird. — (A. S. *wyrd.*) Destiny, Fate; so frequently used of Fate personified, and of Destiny in general; the Ruler of human destiny. Perhaps a remnant of the heathen mythology visible in the use of this word, under the Christian coloring of the poem.

BEOWULF.

————∘∘⦂⊛⦂∘∘————

BEOWULF AND GRENDEL.

I.

Scyld and his descendants. Hrothgar and the building of
Heorot. The coming of Grendel, and his evil deeds.
Hrothgar's great sorrow.

I. L O ! we of the Spear-Danes', in days of yore,
Warrior-kings' glory have heard,
How the princes heroic deeds wrought.
Oft Scyld, son of Scef, from hosts of foes,

5 From many tribes, their mead-seats took;
The earl caused terror since first he was
Found thus forlorn: gained he comfort for that,
Grew under the clouds, in honors throve,
Until each one of those dwelling around

10 Over the whale-road, him should obey,
Should tribute pay: that was a good king !
To him was a son afterwards born,
Young in his palace, one whom God sent
To the people for comfort: their distress He perceived

15 That they ere suffered life-eating care
So long a while.   Him therefor life's Lord,
King of glory, world-honor gave:
Beowulf was noted (wide spread his fame),
The son of Scyld in Scedelands.

20 So shall a young man with presents cause,
With rich money-gifts in his father's house,
That him in old age may after attend

Willing comrades; when war shall come,
May stand by their chief; by deeds of praise shall
25 In every tribe a hero thrive !
  Then Scyld departed at the hour of fate,
  The warlike to go into his Lord's keeping :
  They him then bore to the ocean's wave,
  His trusty comrades, as he himself bade,
30 Whilst with words ruled the friend of the Scyldings,
  Belovéd land-prince ; long wielded he power.
  There stood at haven with curvéd prow,
  Shining and ready, the prince's ship :
  The people laid their dear war-lord,
35 Giver of rings, on the deck of the ship,
  The mighty by th' mast.   Many treasures were there,
  From distant lands, ornaments brought ;
  Ne'er heard I of keel more comelily filled
  With warlike weapons and weeds of battle,
40 With bills and burnies !   On his bosom lay
  A heap of jewels, which with him should
  Into the flood's keeping afar depart :
  Not at all with less gifts did they him provide,
  With princely treasures, than those had done,
45 Who him at his birth had erst sent forth
  Alone o'er the sea when but a child.
  Then placed they yet a golden standard
  High over his head, let the waves bear
  Their gift to the sea ; sad was their soul,
50 Mourning their mood.   Men indeed cannot
  Say now in sooth, hall-possessors,
  Heroes 'neath heavens, who that heap took.
  II. Then was in the cities Beowulf, the Scyldings'
  Belovéd folk-king, for a long time
55 Renowned 'mid the nation (elsewhere went his father
  The prince from his home), till from him after sprang
  The great Healfdene : he ruled while he lived,

Agéd and warlike, kindly the Scyldings.
To him were four children, reckoned in order,
60 Born into the world, to the prince of the people,
Heorogar and Hrothgar and Halga the good.
I heard that Elan wife of Ongentheow was,
The warlike Scylfing's bed-companion.
Then was to Hrothgar war-speed given,
65 Honor in battle, that him his dear kinsmen
Gladly obeyed, until the youth grew,
A great band of men.   It came into his mind
That he a great hall would then command,
A greater mead-hall his men to build
70 Than children of men ever had heard of,
And there within would he all deal out
To young and to old, as God him gave,
Except the folk-land and lives of men.
Then far and wide heard I the work was ordered
75 To many a tribe throughout this mid-earth
The folk-hall to deck.   Him in time it befell
Quickly with men, that it was all ready,
The greatest of halls : Heort as name gave he it,
He who with his word power far and wide had.
80 He belied not his promise, bracelets he dealt,
Treasure at banquet.   The hall arose
Lofty and pinnacled ; hostile waves it awaited
Of hateful fire.   Nor was it yet long
Before fierce hatred to the frightened men,
85 For deadly enmity, was to arise,
  Since the fell spirit most spitefully
For a time endured, who in darkness abode,
That he on each day the sound of joy heard
Loud in the hall : there was harp's sound,
90 Clear song of the minstrel.   He said, he who could
The creation of men from of old relate,
Quoth that the Almighty the earth had wrought,

The beautiful plain which water surrounds,
Victorious had set the sun and the moon
95 As lights for light to the land-dwellers,
And had adorned the regions of earth
With limbs and leaves. life also created
For every kind of living beings.
Thus were the warriors living in joys
100 Happily then, until one began
Great woes to work, a fiend of hell:
The wrathful spirit was Grendel named,
The mighty mark-stepper who the moors held,
Fen and fastness: the sea-fiend's abode
105 The joyless being a while in-dwelt,
Since the Creator him had proscribed.
(Upon Cain's kin that crime avenged
The Lord eternal, for that he slew Abel:
Joyed he not in that feud, but him afar banished
110 For that crime the Creator away from mankind:
Thence evil demons all were produced,
Eotens and elves and monsters of sea,
Such were the giants who strove against God
For a long time: He repaid them for that.)
115 III. Then went he to seek out, after night came,
The high-built house, how the Ring-Danes,
After their beer-feast, it had arranged.
He found then therein a band of nobles
Asleep after feasting: sorrows they knew not,
120 Misfortunes of men. The demon of death,
Grim and greedy, soon was ready,
Fierce and furious, and in rest took
Thirty of thanes; thence back he departed,
Exulting in booty, homeward to go,
125 With this fill of slaughter to seek out his dwelling.
Then at early morn was with dawn of day
Grendel's war-craft made known to men:

Then after his meal was wailing upraised,
A great morning-cry: the mighty prince,
130 The honored chief, sorrowful sat,
The strong man suffered, thane-sorrow endured,
After the foeman's footsteps they beheld,
The cursed demon's: too severe was that sorrow,
Loathsome and lasting.   No longer time was it,
135 But after one night he again wrought
More deeds of murder, and did not shrink from
Hatred and evil: too firm he was in them.
Then was easy to find one who elsewhere,
Farther removed, rest for himself sought,
140 A bed next the chambers, since to him was shown,
Truly was said by a manifest sign
The hall-thane's hatred: he held himself after
Further and firmer, who 'scaped from the fiend.
So then he reigned and strove against right
145 Alone against all, until empty stood
The finest of houses.   Long was the time:
Twelve winters' time suffering endured
The friend of the Scyldings, each one of woes,
Of sorrows extreme: therefore was this misery
150 Openly known to the children of men,
Sadly in songs, that Grendel contended
A while against Hrothgar, hateful war waged,
Evil and enmity many half-years,
Contests continual; peacefully would not
155 From any one man of the might of the Danes
Life-bale remove, nor with money compound;
No one of the wise men need there expect
A ransom more splendid at the murderer's hands
The terrible demon harassing was,
160 Dark death-shadow, the old and the young,
Caught and entrapped them; in constant night held
The misty moors: men know not indeed

Whither hell's demons wander in crowds.
So many foul deeds the foe of mankind,
165 The terrible lone one, often enacted,
Direful afflictions ; Heorot he dwelt in,
The costly-decked hall, on the dark nights ;
Yet must he not the rich gift-stool approach
For the Creator, nor wish for it know.
170 That was great sorrow of the friend of the Scyldings,
Misery of mind ! Many oft sat
Mighty in council ; plans they devised,
What with bold mind then would be best
'Gainst the sudden attacks for them to do.
175 Sometimes they vowed at their temples of idols
To their gods worship, with words they prayed
The destroyer of spirits would render them help
Against their folk-sorrows. Such was their custom,
Hope of the heathen : well they remembered
180 In their minds' thoughts ; the Creator they knew not,
Judge of their deeds : the good Lord they knew not,
Heaven's protector could they not praise,
The King of glorÿ. Woe be to him who shall,
Through deadly hate, thrust down his soul
185 Into the fire-abyss ; for comfort he'll hope not,
By no means return ! Well be to him who may,
After his death-day, seek for the Lord,
In the Father's bosom mercy beseech !

II.

*The arrival of Beowulf. His talk with the warden. His
reception by Hrothgar. He makes known his errand.*

IV. So then great sorrow Healfdene's son
190 Continually suffered : might not the wise chieftain
His woes remove : too great was that pain,
Loathsome and lasting, that came on the people,

Dreadful distress, greatest of night-bales.
That from home learnt Higelac's thane,
195 Good 'mong the Geats, the deeds of Grendel:
He was of mankind strongest in might
In the day then of this mortal life,
Noble and great.　For him a ship bade he
A good one prepare, quoth, he the war-king
200 Over the swan-road wished to seek out,
The mighty prince, since he need had of men.
That journey to him the cunning churls
Not at all blamed, though he dear to them was.
They whetted the brave one, good omens they saw.
205 The good one had of the Geats' people
Warriors chosen, of those whom he bravest
Was able to find: one of fifteen
The vessel he sought: a warrior made known,
A sea-crafty man, the ..eighboring landmarks.
210 Thus time went on: on the waves was the ship,
Boat under the mountain.　The heroes ready
On the prow stied: the billows rolled
The sea 'gainst the sand.　The warriors bore
On the deck of the ship ornaments bright,
215 Equipments ornate: the men shoved out,
Men on willing journey, the well-fitted wood.
Went then o'er the waves, by the wind hastened,
The foamy-necked float to a fowl most like,
Till at the same hour of the following day
220 The curvéd prow had traversed the water,
So that the sailors then saw the land,
The sea-cliffs shine, the mountains steep,
The broad sea-nesses.　Then was the sea-goer
At the end of its voyage.　Thence quickly up
225 The Weders' people on the plain stied,
The sea-wood tied, their battle-sarks rattled,
Their weeds of war: thanked they then God

That for them the sea-paths easy were found.
Then saw from the wall the guard of the Scyldings,
230 He who the sea-cliffs was set to hold,
Bear o'er the bulwarks bright-looking shields,
Weapons ready for war: wonder aroused him
In his mind's thoughts as to what these men were.
Went he then to the sea on his steed riding,
235 The thane of Hrothgar; with might he shook
The strong wood in his hands, with formal words
     spoke:
"What now are ye of arms-bearing men
With burnies protected, who thus a high keel
Over the sea-path bringing have come
240 O'er the waves hither, clad in helmets?
I was the coast-guard, sea-watch I kept
That no one of foes on the Danes' land
With a ship-army injury might do.
Not here more openly ever have come
245 Bearers of shields!   Ye the permission
Of warlike men did not well know,
Consent of kinsmen!   Ne'er saw I a greater
Earl upon earth than is one of you,
A hero in armor: that is no home-stayer
250 With weapons adorned, unless looks belie him,
His peerless appearance.   Now I of you shall
The origin learn, ere ye far hence,
Like to false spies, in the land of the Danes
Further advance.   Now ye far-dwelling,
255 Sea-faring men, give willing ear
To my simple thought: haste now is best
To make plainly known whence is your coming."
V. To him then the princely one quickly replied,
The war-band's leader his word-hoard unlocked:
260 "We are of the race of the Geats' people,
And are of Hygelac hearth-companions.

My own father was well-known to the folk,
A princely ruler, Ecgtheow called:
Many winters he lived ere he away went
265 Aged from his dwelling: him well remembers
Each one of the wise men wide through the earth.
With friendly mind we thine own lord,
Healfdene's son, seeking are come,
The people's protector.   Be thou our informant.
270 We have to the mighty a mickle errand,
To the lord of the Danes: nor shall aught be hidden
Of this, as I think.   Thou knowest, if it is,
As we indeed truly have heard it said,
That 'mong the Scyldings I know not what foe,
275 A secret enemy, on the dark nights,
Shows by his terror hatred unknown,
Oppression and slaughter.   I for that Hrothgar
With kindly mind counsel may give,
How he, old and good, shall the foe overcome,
280 If yet for him ever should cease
The misery of woes, release again come,
And the care-waves cooler become;
Or ever hereafter a time of trouble,
Oppression he'll suffer, while there remains
285 In its high place the noblest of houses."
The warden spoke, where on his horse sat
The fearless warrior: "Of each of these shall
A wise shield-warrior the difference know,
Of words and works, he who well judgeth.
290 I that do hear, that this band is friendly
To the lord of the Scyldings; go then forth bearing
Your weapons and war-weeds; I shall direct you:
Likewise my war-thanes I shall command
Against any foe this vessel of yours,
295 The newly-tarred boat, on the sea-sand
With honor to hold, till back shall bear

O'er the sea-waves the friendly man
The curved-prowed craft to Wedermark.
To such a good-doer will it be granted,
300 That this battle-storm he safe shall escape."
Then journeyed they on: the boat remained still,
In the bay rested the broad-bosomed ship,
At anchor fast. The boar's likeness shone:
Over the visor, with gold adorned,
305 Bright and fire-hardened, the boar kept guard.
The fierce-minded hurried, the heroes hastened,
Together they went, till the well-built hall,
Shining and gold-adorned, they might perceive:
That was the foremost to dwellers on earth
310 Of halls under heavens, in which the king dwelt;
The light from it shone o'er many of lands.
To them then the warrior the court of the proud
Glittering showed, that they to it might
Straightway proceed, one of war-heroes:
315 Turned he his horse, his word then spoke:
"My time 'tis to go. May the Father Almighty
With His gracious favor you now preserve
Safe on your journey! I will at the sea
'Gainst hostile band keep guard of the coast."
320 VI. The road was stone-laid, the path directed
The men together. The war-burnie shone,
Hard and hand-locked, the bright ringéd-iron
Sang in the armor, when they to the hall
In their war-weeds at first approached.
325 Sea-wearied they set their broad-shapen shields,
Their stout-made bucklers, against the hall's wall,
Went then to the benches; their burnies rang,
War-armor of men; their long spears stood,
The sea-men's weapons, all together,
330 Grey ash-shaft above; the armored band was
With weapons adorned. There then a bold warrior

Inquired of the heroes concerning their kinship:
"Whence do ye bear your gilded shields,
Gray-colored sarks and grim-looking helmets,
335 Heap of war-shafts? I am of Hrothgar
Attendant and servant. Ne'er saw I strangers,
So many men, with prouder looks.
I think ye for valor, and not in exile,
But for high-mindedness Hrothgar have sought."
340 Him then the hero famed-for-strength answered,
The brave Weders' prince, his word then spoke,
Bold under his helmet: "We are of Hygelac
Table-companions, Beowulf's my name.
I wish to tell to the son of Healfdene,
345 The illustrious prince, my errand to him,
Thy lord, and to know if he will us grant
That we him so good friendly may greet."
Wulfgar then spoke (he was Vandals' chief,
His strength of mind was to many well-known,
350 His prowess and wisdom): "I the Danes' friend,
The lord of the Scyldings, therefore will ask,
The giver of rings, as thou art a suppliant,
The illustrious prince, concerning thy errand,
And to thee the answer at once will announce,
355 Which to me the good one thinketh to give."
Went he then quickly to where Hrothgar sat,
Old and gray-headed, with his band of earls;
The warlike went, till he stood in the presence
Of the lord of the Danes; he knew the court's custom.
360 Wulfgar then spoke to his own dear lord:
"Here are arrived, come from afar
Over the sea-waves, men of the Geats;
The one most distinguished the warriors brave
Beowulf name. They are thy suppliants
365 That they, my prince, may with thee now
Greetings exchange: do not thou refuse them

Thy converse in turn, friendly Hrothgar!
They in their war-weeds seem very worthy
Contenders with earls: the chief is renowned
370 Who these war-heroes hither has led."
VII. Hrothgar then spoke, defence of the Scyldings:
"I knew him of old when he was a child:
His agéd father was Ecgtheow named;
To him at home gave Hrethel the Geat
375 His only daughter: his son has now
Boldly come here, a trusty friend sought.
Then this was said by the sea-farers,
Those who did tribute for the Geats carry
Thither for favor, that he thirty men's
380 Great strength of might in his hand-grip,
Brave in war, has. Him holy God
For gracious help to us has sent,
To the West-Danes, as I have hope,
Against Grendel's terror: I shall to the good one
385 For his boldness of mind costly gifts offer.
Be thou in haste, bid them come in,
A friendly band see all together!
Tell them too in words that they are welcome
To the Danes' people."— [To the hall-door
390 Wulfgar then went], words within spoke:
"To you bade me say my victor-lord,
Prince of the East-Danes, that your kinship he
    knows,
And ye are to him over the sea-waves,
Bold-minded men, welcome hither.
395 Now ye may go in your war-armor,
Under your helmets, Hrothgar to see:
Let ye your battle-shields here then await,
Your spears, deadly shafts, the converse of words."
Then rose the mighty, many warriors around him,
400 A brave band of thanes: some there abode,

The battle-weeds kept, as them the chief bade.
They hastened together, as the guide them directed,
Under Heorot's roof: the valiant one went
Bold under his helmet, till he in the hall stood.
405 Beowulf spoke (on him shone the burnie,
The linkéd net-work forged by the smith's craft) :
"Be thou, Hrothgar, hail! I am of Hygelac
Kinsman and war-thane : many exploits have I
Undertaken in youth.   To me Grendel's deed
410 In my native land clearly was known :
The sea-farers say that this mead-hall stands,
Noblest of halls, for each one of heroes
Empty and useless, when even-light
In the brightness of heaven has been concealed.
415 Then did my people give me advice,
The noblest of men, craftiest of churls,
Princely Hrothgar, that I thee should seek ;
For that they knew my own strength of might :
They themselves saw when I came from the battle,
420 Blood-stained from my foes, where sea-monsters I
        bound,
The eoten-race killed, and on the waves slew
The nickers by night, endured great distress,
Avenged Weders' sorrows (woes had they suffered),
Their foe-men destroyed, and now against Grendel,
425 Against the dread monster, alone shall decide
The fight 'gainst the giant.   I of thee now then,
Prince of the Bright-Danes, desire to make,
Chief of the Scyldings, but one request, —
That do not thou refuse me, defender of warriors,
430 Dear friend of the people, now thus far am I come, —
That I may alone and my band of earls,
This company brave, Heorot cleanse.
Also have I heard that the dread monster
For boldness of mood recks not for weapons :

435 I that then do scorn — so be to me Hygelac,
My own people's-king, gracious in mind —
That I a sword bear or a broad shield
Yellow-rimmed to the battle; but I with grip shall
'Gainst my foe grapple and for life strive
440 Foe against foe: there shall confide
In the doom of the Lord he whom death takes.
I ween that he will, if he may prevail,
In the war-hall the folk of the Geats,
The fearless, devour, as he oft did
445 The might of the Hrethmen; thou needest not then
My head conceal, but me he will have
Stainéd with gore, if death me take,
My bloody corpse bear, think to devour it,
Will eat it alone, unpityingly,
450 Will mark the moor-mounds: thou needest not then
For my body's food longer take care.
Send thou to Hygelac, if battle me take,
Best one of war-weeds that covers my breast,
Noblest of burnies; 'tis Hraedla's bequest,
455 Weland's skilled work. Goes aye Weird as it will!"
VIII. Hrothgar then spoke, defence of the Scyldings:
" For fight of protection, Beowulf my friend,
And for assistance, hast thou us sought.
Thy father fought a mighty contest;
460 He was of Heatholaf the slayer by hand
Among the Wylfings, when the kin of the Waras
'Gainst the terror of war him might not have.
After that sought he the South-Danes' folk
· Over the sea-waves, the Honor-Scyldings,
465 When I first ruled the folk of the Danes,
And in youth held the jewelled-rich
Hoard-city of heroes, when Heregar was dead,
My elder brother bereft of life,
The son of Healfdene; he was better than I.

470 Afterwards the feud with money I settled ;
  I sent to the Wylfings o'er the waters' ridge
  Old-time treasures ; he swore to me oaths.
  Sorrow is in my mind for me to say
  To any of men what to me Grendel hath
475 Of harm in Heorot with his hateful thoughts,
  Of sudden woes wrought ; my hall-band is,
  My war-heap, vanished ; Weird swept them away
  Into Grendel's terror.   God easily may
  The mad foe restrain from his evil deeds.
480 Very often they boasted, drunken with beer,
  Over the ale-cup, the warriors bold,
  That they in the beer-hall would then await
  Grendel's contest with their terrible swords.
  Then was this mead-hall in the morning-time,
485 Lordly hall, stained with gore, when day-light shone.
  All the bench-rows covered with blood,
  The hall with sword-gore ; I had the less lieges,
  Dearest companions, whom death took away.
  Sit now at the feast and free from court-rules
490 The heroes victorious, as pleases thy mind."
  Then was for the Geat-men all together
  In the beer-hall a bench prepared,
  Where the bold-minded hastened to sit,
  Proud in their strength.   The thane did his service,
495 Who in his hands bore a gold-adorned ale-cup,
  Poured out the clear mead. Sometimes sang the
   · minstrel
  With clear voice in Heorot : there was joy of heroes,
  No little band of Danes and Weders.

III.

Hunferth's taunt.   The swimming-match with Breca.   Joy in Heorot.

IX. Hunferth then spoke, the son of Ecglaf,
500 Who at the feet sat of the lord of the Scyldings,
    Unloosed his war-secret (was the coming of Beowulf,
    The proud sea-farer, to him mickle grief,
    For that he granted not that any man else
    Ever more honor of this mid-earth
505 Should gain under heavens than he himself) :
    "Art thou that Beowulf who strove with Breca
    On the broad sea in swimming-match,
    When ye two for pride the billows tried
    And for vain boasting in the deep water
510 Riskéd your lives?   You two no man,
    Nor friend nor foe, might then dissuade
    From sorrowful venture, when ye on the sea swam,
    When ye the sea-waves with your arms covered,
    Measured the sea-ways, struck with your hands,
515 Glided o'er ocean ; with its great billows
    Welled up winter's flood.   In the power of the waters
    Ye seven nights strove : he in swimming thee con-
       quered,
    He had greater might.   Then him in the morning
    On the Heathoremes' land the ocean bore up,
520 Whence he did seek his pleasant home,
    Dear to his people, the land of the Brondings·
    His fair strong city, where he had people,
    A city and rings.   All his boast against thee
    The son of Beanstan truly fulfilled.
· 525 Then ween I for thee a worse result,
    Though thou in battle wert everywhere good,
    A fiercer fight, if thou Grendel darest

The space of one night nigh to abide."
Beowulf spoke, Ecgtheow's son :
530 " Lo ! thou very much, Hunferth my friend,
Drunken with beer, hast spoken of Breca,
Hast said of his journey.   I say the truth,
That I did the more sea-power possess,
Endurance 'mid waves, than any man else.
535 We two said this, when we were boys,
And we of this boasted (both were then still
In the prime of youth), that we out on the sea
Our lives would risk ; and that we accomplished.
A naked sword had we, when we swam on the sea,
540 Boldly in hand : ourselves 'gainst the whales
We thought to defend.   Not at all from me
On the flood-waves could he afar float,
On the sea quicker ; I from him would not.
Then we two together were in the sea
545 The space of five nights, till flood apart drove us,
The swelling billows, coldest of storms,
Darkening night, and the north wind
Boisterous and fierce ; rough were the waves.
The sea-fishes' spirit was then aroused :
550 There 'gainst the foes my body-sark,
Hard and hand-locked, to me help afforded ;
The braided war-burnie on my breast lay,
With gold adorned.   To the bottom me drew
The hostile foe ; he held me fast,
555 Grim in his grip ; yet was it granted me,
That I the monster with sword-point reached,
With battle-brand : the struggle took off
The mighty mere-beast by my own hand.
X. "So often upon me the hateful foes
560 Powerfully pressed : I punished them
With my dear sword, as it behooved me.
Not at all did they have joy of their meal,

The evil-doers, that they me might devour,
'Round their banquet might sit nigh the sea-bottom,
565 But in the morning wounded with swords
Around the sea-strand and upon it they lay,
With swords put to sleep, that never thereafter
Upon the high ocean the farers-by-sea
Might they let on their journey. Light from the east
　　came,
570 Bright beacon of God : still were the waves,
So that I the sea-nesses might now behold,
The windy walls. Weird often preserves
An unfated earl, when his might has availed !
Yet it granted to me that I with sword slew
575 Nine of the nickers. Ne'er heard I at night
Under heaven's vault of a harder fight,
Nor on the sea-billows of a more wretched man :
Yet I my foes' grip with life escaped
Weary of th' journey. Then me the sea bore,
580 The flood o'er the waves, upon the Finns' land,
The welling waters. Not at all about thee
Of such-like contests have I heard tell,
Of terror with swords. Breca ne'er yet
In battle-play, nor either of you,
585 So daring a deed ever has done,
With stainéd swords (not of that do I boast),
Though thou thine own brothers' murderer wast,
Thy blood-relations' : for this shalt thou in hell
Curses endure, though thy wit may avail !
590 I tell thee in truth, son of Ecglaf,
That never had Grendel wrought so many horrors,
The terrible monster, to thine own prince,
Shame in Heorot, if thy mind were,
Thy temper, so fierce, as thou thyself reckonest :
595 But he hath found that he the feud need not,
The terrible contest of your own people,

Very much dread, of the Victor-Scyldings ;
He taketh forced pledge, he spareth no one
Of the Danes' people, but he joy beareth,
600 Killeth and eateth, nor weeneth of contest
With the Spear-Danes.   But I to him shall
The Geats' strength and might without delay now
Offer in battle.   Then shall go he who may
Proudly to mead, when morning-light
605 Of the second day o'er the children of men,
The sun ether-clad, shall shine from the South."
Then was in joy the giver of treasure,
Gray-haired and war-fierce ; help he expected,
The ruler of Bright-Danes ; in Beowulf heard
610 The people's shepherd the firm-set purpose.
There was laughter of heroes, the harp merry
     sounded,
Winsome were words.   Went Wealhtheow forth,
The queen of Hrothgar, mindful of courtesies,
Gold-adorned greeted the men in the hall,
615 And the high-born woman then gave the cup
First to the East-Danes' home-protector,
Bade him be blithe at the beer-drinking,
Him dear to his people.   In joy he received
The food and the hall-cup, victorious king.
620 Then around went the Helmings' lady
To every division of old and of young,
Costly gifts gave, until the time came
That she to Beowulf, the ring-adorned queen,
Noble in mind, the mead-cup bore :
625 She greeted the Geats' chief, thanks gave to God,
Wise in her words, that the wish to her fell,
That on any earl she might rely
For comfort in evils.   Received he the cup,
The warrior fierce, at Wealhtheow's hands.
630 And then he spoke, ready for battle ;

Beowulf spoke, Ecgtheow's son:
"This thought I then, when I on the sea stied,
Boarded my sea-boat with my warrior-band,
That I throughout of your own people
635 The will would work, or in battle fall,
Fast in fiend's grip. I shall perform
Deeds of valor, or end-day mine
In this mead-hall I shall await."
To the woman these words well-pleasing were,
640 Boasts of the Geat: gold-adorned went
The high-born queen to sit by her lord.
Then was as before again in the hall
Mighty word spoken, in joy were the people,
The victor-folk's shout, until all at once
645 The son of Healfdene wished to seek out
His evening-rest; he knew for the monster
In the high hall was battle prepared,
647ᵃ [Because in this hall the Ring-Danes never
647ᵇ Dared to abide unless by day-time],
From the time that they the sun-light might see,
Till night spreading darkness over all things,
650 Night-wandering spirits, came advancing
Dark under the clouds. The crowd all arose:
Greeted then glad-minded one man another,
Hrothgar Beowulf, and offered him hail,
Power o'er the mead-hall, and this word spoke:
655 "Never to any man ere did I trust,
Since I could lift my hand and my shield,
Royal hall of the Danes except to thee now.
   · Have now and hold the noblest of houses,
Of glory be mindful, a hero's might show,
660 Watch 'gainst the foe. No wish shalt thou want,
If thou the great struggle escapest with life."

IV.

*Beowulf and his men occupy Heorot. The coming of
Grendel.   The mighty contest.   Beowulf's victory.*

XI. Then Hrothgar went with his warrior-band,
    The prince of the Scyldings, out of the hall:
    The war-prince would Wealhtheow seek,
665 His queen as companion.   The glory of kings
    Grendel against, as men heard say,
    A hall-guard had set: he performed special service
    For the prince of the Danes, he eoten-guard kept.
    Now the prince of the Geats earnestly trusted
670 In his proud might, in the Creator's favor.
    Then he laid him aside his iron burnie,
    Helmet from head, his jewelled sword gave,
    Choicest of weapons, to his servant-thane,
    And bade him keep his armor of war.
675 Then spoke the hero some boastful words,
    Beowulf the Geat, ere he on bed stied:
    "I count not myself less good in war-might
    For deeds of battle than Grendel himself:
    Therefore with my sword I him will not kill,
680 Of life deprive, though I it all may.
    He knows not these goods, so that he me may slay,
    Hew down my shield, although he be fierce
    In hostile deeds: but we at night shall
    From swords refrain, if he dare to seek
685 War without weapons; and then the wise God,
    The holy Lord, on whatever hand
    May the glory adjudge, as seems to Him fit."
    Then lay down the warlike: the pillow received
    The cheeks of the earl, and him around many
690 A valiant sea-warrior sought his hall-rest.
    No one of these thought that thence he should

Again his dear home ever seek out,
Folk or free-city where he was reared ;
But they had heard that too many before
695 In this wine-hall bloody death carried off
Of the folk of the Danes.   But to them the Lord gave
The web of war-speed, to the folk of the Weders
Comfort and help, so that they their foes
Through the craft of one all overcame,
700 By the might of one self : the truth is made known
That the mighty God the race of man
Has always ruled. — Came in wan night
The shadow-goer stepping.   The warriors slept,
Who the horned hall then were to hold,
705 All except one.   That was to men known,
That them he might not, whom the Creator would not,
The hostile demon drag into darkness ;
But he keeping watch for his foe in anger
Awaited enraged the result of the battle.
710 XII. Then came from the moor 'neath the misty
          slopes
Grendel going, God's anger he bore.
The wicked foe thought of the race of man
Some one to entrap in that high hall :
He went 'neath the clouds whither he the wine-hall,
715 The gold-hall of men, most thoroughly knew,
Shining with gold-plates : that was not the first time
That he of Hrothgar the home had sought.
Ne'er in his life-time before nor after
Bolder warriors, hall-thanes, did he find !
720 Then came to the hall the being approaching,
Of joys deprived.   The door soon sprang open
Fast in its fire-bands, when he with hands touched it ;
Then burst the bale-bringer, since he was enraged,
The door of the hall.   Soon after that
725 On the many-colored floor the fiendish one trod,

Mad in mind went: from his eyes stood
A loathsome light likest to flame.
He saw in the hall many of warriors,
A band in peace sleeping all together,
730 A heap of kin-warriors.   Then laughed his mood,
He thought that he would, ere day came, divide,
The terrible monster, of every one
The life from the body, since to him was fallen
A hope of much food.   That no longer was fated,
735 That he might more of the race of man
Devour by night.   The strong-in-might saw,
The kinsman of Hygelac, how the fell foe
With his swift attacks was going to act.
That did not the monster think to delay,
740 But quickly he seized for the first time
A sleeping warrior, him tore unresisting,
Bit his bone-frame, drank blood from his veins,
In great bites him swallowed: soon then he had,
Deprived of life, him all devoured,
745 Feet even and hands.   Forth nearer he stepped,
Seized then with his hands the firm-in-mind
Warrior at rest.   Him reached out against
The fiend with his hand: quickly he seized
The cunning-in-mind and on his arm sat.
750 Soon this perceived the worker of evil,
That he never found in this mid-earth,
In the regions of earth, in another man
A greater hand-grip: in mood he became
In his soul frightened; he could not sooner forth.
755 His mind was death-ready; into darkness would flee,
The devil-band seek: his course was not there,
As he in old-days before had found.
Remembered he then, good kinsman of Hygelac,
His evening-speech; upright he stood
760 And him fast seized: his fingers cracked.

The eoten would outwards : the earl further stepped ;
The mighty one thought, whereso he might,
Afar to escape, and away thence
Flee into the marshes : he knew that his fingers
765 Were in his foe's grip : that was a bad journey
That the harm-bringing foe had taken to Heorot :
The royal hall sounded : for all the Danes was,
The city-dwellers, each one of the bold,
For earls the ale spilt. Angry were both
770 Furious contestants : the hall cracked aloud :
Then was it great wonder that the wine-hall
Withstood the fierce fighters, that it to ground fell
    not,
The fair folk-hall : but it was too fast
Within and without in its iron bands
775 By cunning skill forged. There from the sill fell
Many a mead-bench, as I have heard say,
Adorned with gold, where the foes fought.
Of this before weened not wise men of the Scyldings
That it ever with strength any of men,
780 Goodly and bone-adorned, to pieces might break,
With craft destroy, unless flame's embrace
In smoke should it swallow. The sound arose
Often repeated : to the North-Danes stood
Fearful terror, to every one
785 Of those who from the wall the weeping heard,
The terrible song sung of th' opposer of God,
The joyless song, his pain lament
The prisoner of hell. He held him too fast,
He who of men was strongest in might
790 In the day then of this mortal life.
XIII. The earl's defence would on no account
The bringer of woes let go alive,
Nor his life-days to any people
Did he count useful. There brandished many

795 An earl of Beowulf his good old sword ;
    His dear lord's life he would defend,
    His noble chief's, whereso they might ;
    They knew not indeed, when they risked the contest,
    The bold-in-mind heroes of battle,
800 And on each side they thought to hew,
    To seek his soul, that the fiendish demon
    Not any on earth choicest of weapons,
    No one of war-swords, was able to touch,
    But he had forsworn victorious weapons,
805 Each one of swords.   His life-leaving should,
    In the day then of this mortal life,
    Miserably happen, and the strange-spirit
    Into his foes' power afar depart.
    Then that he perceived, he who oft before
810 In mirth of mind against mankind
    His crimes had wrought, hostile to God,
    That his body's frame him would not sustain,
    But him the proud kinsman of Hygelac
    Had by the hands : each was to other
815 Living a foe.   Pain of body endured
    The terrible monster : there was on his shoulder
    An evident wound ; apart sprang the sinews,
    The bone-frame burst.   To Beowulf was
    Battle-fame given : Grendel should thence
820 Sick-of-life flee under the fen-slopes,
    Seek his joyless abode ; too surely he knew
    That of his life the end was come,
    The span of his days.   To all of the Danes
    By the bloody strife was the wish fulfilled ;
825 He then had cleansed, who ere came from afar,
    Wise and valiant, the hall of Hrothgar,
    Saved it from sorrow, rejoiced in his night-work,
    His glorious deeds. . Then for the East-Danes
    The prince of the Geats his boast had performed,

830   Likewise the sufferings all had removed,
     Sorrows from foe, which they ere suffered,
     And by compulsion had to endure,
     No little distress. That was a clear proof,
     After the battle-brave laid down the hand,
835   The arm and the shoulder (there all was together),
     The claw of Grendel 'neath the wide roof.

V.

Joy of the Danes. The minstrel's song of Sigemund and
Fitela: of Heremod. Hrothgar's thanks to Beowulf.

XIV. Then was in the morning, as I have heard say,
     Around the gift-hall many a warrior:
     The people's leaders from far and near came
840   Through the wide ways the wonder to view,
     The tracks of the foe. Ne'er did his life-severing
     Sorrowful seem to any of men,
     Of those who then viewed the track of the vanquished,
     How weary in mind he away thence,
845   In fight overcome, to the mere of the nickers,
     Doomed and driven, his life-tracks bore.
     There was the surface welling in blood;
     The frightful waves' lashing all commingled
     Hot in gore boiled with the sword-blood;
850   The doomed-to-death dyed them, when of joys de-
         prived
     In his fen-refuge he laid down his life,
     His heathen soul, where hell him received.
     Thence back again came the old companions,
     And many a young one from their glad course,
855   From the sea proudly riding on horses,
     Heroes on steeds. There then was Beowulf's

Glory proclaimed : oft many said
That south nor north by the two seas
O'er the wide earth no other one
860 'Neath heaven's expanse was better than he
Of bearers of shields, more worthy of rule.
They did not now at all their dear lord blame,
The friendly Hrothgar, but that was a good king.
Sometimes the battle-famed permitted to leap,
865 In contest to go, their yellow horses
Where the land-roads seemed to them fair,
Known for their goodness. Sometimes a king's thane,
A man renowned, mindful of songs,
He who very many of old-time sagas,
870 A great number remembered, framed other words
Rightly connected : the scope then began
Beowulf's exploit with skill to tell,
And with art to relate well-composed tales,
Words to exchange ; he told everything
875 That he of Sigemund had heard men say,
His noble deeds, much of the unknown,
The Waelsing's contest, his journeys wide,
Which the children of men did not well know,
The feuds and crimes, but Fitela with him,
880 When he some such thing wished to relate,
Uncle to nephew, as they ever were
In every fight comrades in need :
They had very many of the race of the eotens
Slain with their swords. To Sigemund came
885 After his death-day no little fame
Since he, brave in war, destroyed the dragon,
The guard of the hoard : he 'neath the gray stone,
The prince's son, had risked alone
The very bold deed ; not with him was Fitela ;
890 Yet it happened to him that the sword pierced
  through

The wonderful worm, that it in the wall stood,
The lordly weapon; in death lay the dragon.
The terrible one in strength had prevailed,
So that he the ring-hoard himself might enjoy
895 At his own will; he loaded his vessel,
Bore on the ship's bosom the ornaments bright,
The son of Waels; the worm's heat melted *him*.
He was of exiles the greatest by far
Among the nations, the warriors' defence
900 In noble deeds; for that ere had he glory.
After of Heremod the battle-might failed,
His strength and prowess, he was 'mong the Jutes
Into his foe's power forthwith betrayed,
Sent away quickly: him waves of sorrow
905 Too long oppressed; he was to his people,
To all of his princes, a life-long distress:
Likewise oft lamented in former times
The brave one's journey many a wise churl,
Who trusted in him for help in misfortunes,
910 That the son of their prince was to grow up,
Take the place of his father, his people possess,
Hoard and head-city, kingdom of heroes,
Home of the Scyldings. *He* was there to all,
The kinsman of Hygelac, to the race of man,
915 To friends more beloved: *him* sorrow befell.—
Sometimes contending the yellow roads
With their horses they measured. Then was morn·
    ing-light
Advanced and hastened: many a man went,
Brave now in mind, to the high hall
920 To see the rare wonder; the king himself also
From his bridal chamber, guardian of treasures,
Stepped strong in glory with a great crowd,
Famed for his virtues, and his queen with him
Measured the mead-path with her maiden-band.

925 XV. Hrothgar then spoke (he went to the hall,
Stood by the column, looked at the high roof
Adorned with gold and at Grendel's hand):
" For this glad sight thanks to the Almighty
Quickly be given ! Much evil I suffered,
930 Sorrows from Grendel : God may ever work
Wonder on wonder, King of glory.
Lately it was that I for myself
Of any of woes weened not my life long
Relief to obtain, since stained with blood
935 The noblest of houses drenched in gore stood ;
Woe was brought down on every wise man,
Of those who weened not that they in their lives
The people's land-work from foes might defend,
From demons and devils.   Now hath a hero,
940 Through the Lord's might, a deed performed,
Which we all before were not at all able
With wisdom to work.   Lo ! this may say
Even whatever woman brought forth this son
After man's nature, if she yet liveth,
945 That to her the eternal Creator was gracious
In her child-bearing.   Now I thee, Beowulf,
Noblest of men, for myself as a son
Will love in life : keep well henceforth
The kinship new.   To thee shall no lack be
950 Of earthly wishes o'er which I have power.
Very often for less have I fixed the reward,
The share of the treasure, to warrior less brave,
One worse in the fight.   Thou hast for thyself
Effected by deeds that thy fame shall live
955 For ever and ever.   May thee the Almighty
With good repay, as He heretofore did !"
Beowulf then spoke, Ecgtheow's son :
" That deed of might we, with great good-will,
That fight have fought, boldly encountered

960 The strength of the unknown: I rather would wish
That thou himself now mightest see,
The foe in his battle-dress wearied to death.
I quickly him with hardest grips
Thought then to bind on the death-bed,
965 That he by hand-grip of mine should lie
Striving for life, if his body escaped not:
I might not him, since the Creator willed not,
Cut off from escape: not so firm held I him,
The life-destroyer: too powerful was he,
970 The foe in his speed.   Yet his hand did he let
For life-protection remain behind,
His arm and shoulder: not there, however,
Did the helpless man gain any comfort.
Not longer shall live the evil-doer
975 Burdened with sins, but him sore pain
In his strong grip sternly has seized,
In his bonds of bale: there shall abide
The sin-stained man the mickle doom,
How the glorious Creator to him will prescribe."
980 Then was more silent the son of Ecglaf
In his boasting-speech of warlike deeds,
After the princes, by the earl's might,
Upon the high roof the hand had viewed,
The foe-man's fingers, each one before him:
985 Each place of the nails was likest to steel,
The heathen's hand-spurs, the battle-monster's
Horrible claw: each one then said
That him would touch of warlike men
No excellent weapon, so that the demon's
990 Bloody war-hand it would break off.

VI.

*Feasting and presents in Heorot. The minstrel's song of
Finn, Hnaef, and Hengest. Wealhtheow's greeting
to Beowulf. All retire to rest.*

XVI. Then quickly was ordered Heorot within
By hands to adorn : there were many of those,
Of men and of women, who that wine-hall,
That guest-room prepared. Gold-adorned shone
995 The webs on the walls, many wondrous sights
To each one of men, who on such look.
That building bright was very much injured,
All the interior in its iron-bands fast ;
The hinges were shivered ; the roof alone saved
1000 Entirely sound, when had the monster,
Condemned for his crimes, in flight escaped,
Hopeless of life. It will not be easy
Fate to escape, let do it who will ;
But each shall obtain of soul-bearing men,
1005 By necessity fixed for the children of men,
For dwellers on earth, the place prepared,
Where his dead body, fast in his death-bed,
Shall sleep after feast. — Then was the fit time
That to the hall went Healfdene's son,
1010 The king himself the feast would enjoy.
Ne'er heard I that folk in greater crowd
Around their ring-giver better behaved.
Went then to the benches the heroes renowned
Rejoiced at the plenty: courteously shared
1015 Many a mead-cup the kinsmen of these,
·The bold-minded ones in the high hall,
Hrothgar and Hrothulf. Heorot within
Was filled with friends : not at all deeds of guile
Did the Folk-Scyldings at this time prepare.

1020 Gave then to Beowulf Healfdene's son
         A golden banner as victory's reward,
         A wreathéd standard, helmet and burnie ;
         A great jewelled sword many then saw
         Before the chief borne.   Beowulf received
1025 The cup in the hall.   Not of that treasure-giving
         Before the warriors need he be ashamed :
         Ne'er heard I, more courteously, that treasures four
         With gold adorned, many of men
         On the ale-bench to each other gave.
1030 'Round the crown of the helmet head-protection
         A boss wound with wires was keeping without,
         That him the battle-swords boldly might not,
         By file hardened, injure, when the shield-warrior
         Against his foes in battle should go.
1035 The earl's defence eight horses ordered,
         With golden trappings, to lead in the hall
         In under the barriers : on one of these stood
         A saddle art-decked, with treasure adorned ;
         That was the battle-seat of the high king,
1040 When in sword-play Healfdene's son
         Wished to engage ; ne'er at the front failed
         The famed one's valor when corpses fell.
         And then to Beowulf of each of the two
         The prince of the Ingwins power delivered,
1045 Of horses and weapons : bade him well use them.
         So like a man the noble prince,
         The hoard-keeper of heroes, contests repaid
         With horses and treasures, such as never will blame
         He who will speak truth according to right.
1050 XVII. Then still on each one the prince of earls,
         Of those who with Beowulf the watery waves trav-
              ersed,
         On the mead-bench a treasure bestowed,
         A sword as an heir-loom, and bade for that one

To pay with gold, whom Grendel before
1055 With evil killed, as he more of them would,
Had not the wise God weird averted,
And the man's courage: the Creator ruled all
Of the race of mankind, as He still doth:
Therefore is insight everywhere best,
1060 Forethought of mind. He shall abide much
Of good and of ill, he who long here
In these days of sorrow useth the world.
There song and music was all together
About Healfdene's battle-leader;
1065 The harp was played, the song oft rehearsed,
When joy in hall Hrothgar's minstrel
Along the mead-bench was to make known:
" He sang of Finn's sons when that danger befell
The heroes of Healfdene, when Hnaef of the Scyldings
1070 In Frisian land was fated to fall.
Then indeed Hildeburh needed not praise
The faith of the Jutes: guiltless was she
Deprived of her dear ones in the shield-play,
Of sons and of brothers: by fate they fell
1075 Wounded with spear: that was a sad woman.
Not without reason did the daughter of Hoc
Lament fate's decree, when morning came,
When she under heaven might then behold
The death-bale of kinsmen, where she before had
1080 Most worldly joy. War took away all
The thanes of Finn except a few only,
So that he could not, on that meeting-place,
In fight with Hengest at all contend,
Nor even the remnant rescue by war
1085 From the chief's thane: but they offered them terms,
That they for them other hall would provide,
Hall and high seat, that they power of half
With the Jutes' sons were to possess,

And at treasure-givings the son of Folcwalda
1090 On every day would honor the Danes,
The hand of Hengest with rings would enrich,
Even as much with costly jewels
Of plated gold, as he the Frisians
In the beer-hall would encourage.
1095 Then they confirmed on either side
A firm peace-compact: Finn to Hengest,
In valor invincible, promised with oaths
That he the remnant, by the doom of his wise men,
In honor would hold, that no man there
1100 By words nor works the compact should break,
Nor ever through cunning should violate it,
Though they their ring-giver's murderer followed,
Deprived of their prince, since so 'twas appointed
 them :
If then of the Frisians any one with bold speech
1105 Of that bloody feud mindful should be,
Then the edge of the sword it should avenge.
The oath was confirmed and treasure of gold
From the hoard taken. Of the warlike Scyldings
The best of the warriors was at the pyre ready ;
1110 At the funeral-pile was easily seen
The blood-stained sark, the all-golden swine,
The boar of hard iron, many a prince
Destroyed by wounds : some fell in slaughter.
Hildeburh bade then at Hnaef's funeral-pyre
1115 To consign to the flame her own dear son,
The body to burn and on the pyre place.
The wretched woman wept on his shoulder,
Mourned him in songs. The fierce smoke arose,
Wound to the clouds the greatest of fires,
1120 Before the mound roared : the heads were melted,
The wound-openings burst ; then out sprang the blood
From the wound of the body. The flame swallowed
 all,

Greediest of spirits, of those whom war took
Of both of the peoples: gone was their breath. —
1125 XVIII. Then went the warriors to visit the dwellings,
Deprived of their friends, Friesland to see,
The homes and high city.   Hengest then still
The slaughter-stained winter dwelt there with Finn,
In valor invincible ; he remembered his land,
1130 Though he might not on the sea drive
The ring-prowed ship : in storm rolled the ocean,
Fought with the wind : winter the waves locked
In its icy bond, until came another
Year in the dwellings, as now still do
1135 (For they ever observe suitable seasons)
The clear-shining days.   Then winter was gone,
Fair was the earth's bosom : strove the exile to go,
The guest from the dwellings ; he then on vengeance
More eagerly thought than on the sea-voyage,
1140 If he might effect a hostile meeting,
And in it remember the sons of the Jutes.
So he did not escape the fate of the world
When Hunlaf's son a battle-sword,
Best of weapons, thrust in his breast ; -
1145 Well-known were its edges among the Jutes.
Also, bold-minded Finn afterwards befell
Death-bringing sword-bale at his own home,
When the fierce battle Guthlaf and Oslaf
After their sea-journey in sorrow lamented,
1150 Blamed him for their woes : his flickering life might
      not
Keep itself in his breast.   Then was the hall covered
With bodies of foes ; also was Finn slain,
The king 'mong his band, and the queen taken.
The Scyldings' warriors bore to their ships
1155 All the possessions of the king of the land,
Such as they might find at Finn's home

Of bright jewels and gems.   They on the sea-road
The royal woman to the Danes bore,
Led to their people."—The song was sung,
1160 The gleeman's glee : the sport then arose.
Carousing resounded : the servants out-poured
Wine from the wondrous vessels.   Then came
 Wealhtheow forth,
Going under her golden crown, where were the good
 ones two
Uncle and nephew sitting : then were they still at peace,
1165 Each one true to the other.   There also the orator
 Hunferth
Sat at the feet of the Scyldings' lord : each of them
 trusted his wisdom,
That he great courage had, tho' to his kinsmen he
 was not
Honest in play of the swords.   Spoke then the queen
 of the Scyldings :
"Receive thou this cup, my dearest lord,
1170 Giver of treasure.   Be thou in health,
Gold-friend of men, and to the Geats speak
With mildest words, as a man shall do.
Be to the Geats kind, mindful of gifts ;
Near and afar hast thou now peace.
1175 One said to me thou for a son would
 · The warrior have.   Heorot is cleansed,
The bright jewel-hall : use whilst thou mayest
Many rewards, and leave to thy kinsmen
Folk and kingdom, when thou shalt forth
1180 Fate's decree see.   I know well indeed
My friendly Hrothulf, that he the youth will
In honor hold, if thou sooner than he,
Friend of the Scyldings, leavest the world :
I ween that he with good will repay
1185 Our own children, if he all remember,

What we, through good-will and also through honor,
Of kindnesses showed to him when a child."
Turned she then to the bench where were her sons,
Hrethric and Hrothmund, and the warriors' children,
1190 The youth together, where sat the good
Beowulf the Geat by the two brothers.
XIX. To him was a cup borne, and friendly greeting
Offered in words, and twisted gold
Gladly presented, arm-ornaments two,
1195 A burnie and rings, the greatest of collars,
Of those which on earth I ever have heard of.
Under the heaven heard I of no better
Hoard-jewel of heroes, since Hama bore
To the bright city the Brosings' collar,
1200 Bright jewel and costly; — he fell into the wiles
Of Eormenric, eternal fate chose.
This ring then had Higelac the Geat,
The grandson of Swerting, the very last time,
When he under his banner defended the treasure,
1205 Battle-spoils guarded: Weird took him away,
When he for pride suffered great woes,
Feud from the Frisians: the jewels he bore,
The precious stones, o'er the wave-holder,
The mighty prince: he fell under his shield,
1210 The life of the king into th' Franks' keeping went,
Breast-battle-weeds and the collar together:
Warriors inferior plundered the slain
After the overthrow of the Geats' people,
The battle-field held. — The hall resounded.
1215 Wealhtheow then said, she before the crowd spoke
"Use this collar, Beowulf dear,
Young man, with joy, and make use of this burnie,
People's treasures, and thrive thou well;
Bear thee with might and be to these youths
1220 Friendly in counsel; thy reward I'll remember.

Thou hast now caused that thee far and near
All thy life long men shall honor,
Even so wide as the sea encircles,
Winds through its walls.   Be, whilst thou livest,
1225 Noble prince, happy.   I grant to thee well
Precious treasures.   Be thou to my sons
Friendly in deeds, thou joyful one :
Here is each earl true to the other,
Mild in his mood, loyal to his liege lord ;
1230 The thanes are at peace, the people all ready ;
Warriors well-drunken, do as I bid."
She went to the seat.   There was choicest of feasts,
The men drank the wine : weird they knew not,
Destiny stern, as it did happen
1235 To many of earls, when even came
And Hrothgar departed to go to his court,
The mighty to rest.   The hall in-dwelt
A number of earls, as they oft before did ;
They emptied the bench-space : it was over-spread
1240 With beds and bolsters.   A certain beer-servant,
Ready and fated, lay down to his rest.
They placed at their heads the battle-shields,
The bright wooden boards : there on the bench was
Over the warrior easily seen
1245 The battle-high helmet, the ringéd burnie,
The mighty spear-shaft ; their custom was
That they often were ready for combat
Both at home and in army, and in each one of them
Even at such a time as to their liege lord
1250 Need there might be : that was a good folk.

VII.

The coming of Grendel's mother.   Sorrow is renewed.
Hrothgar describes the mere.   Beowulf's decision.
His descent into the mere.   The fight with Gren-
del's mother.   Beowulf's return, bearing Grendel's
head.

XX. They went then to sleep: one sorely paid for
    His evening-rest, as to them often happened
    When the gold-hall Grendel in-dwelt,
    Evil deeds wrought, until the end came,
1255 Death for his crimes.   That became plain,
    To men widely known, that still an avenger
    Lived for his foes.   For a long time
    After the war-sorrow Grendel's mother,
    A terrible woman, nourished her grief,
1260 Who was said to inhabit the fearful waters,
    The ice-cold streams, since Cain became
    The murderer by sword of his only brother,
    His father's son; then outlawed he went,
    With murder marked, to flee human joy,
1265 Dwelt in the waste.   Thence many sprang
    Of the demons of fate; of these one was Grendel,
    Hateful and ravenous, who in Heorot found
    A watching man awaiting the battle
    Where the fell monster him was attacking:
1270 Yet he remembered the strength of his might,
    The powerful gift, which God to him gave,
    And on the Lord's favor relied for himself
    For comfort and help: so the fiend overcame he,
    Felled the demon of hell, when he humbled departed,
1275 Deprived of joy, his death-place to see,
    The foe of mankind.   And still his mother,
    Greedy and raging, wished then to go

    The sorrowful journey her son to avenge.
    She came then to Heorot, where the Ring-Danes
1280 Through the hall slept: then there was soon
    A change to the earls, when within entered
    Grendel's mother.   The terror was less
    Even by so much as is woman's strength,
    A woman's war-terror, esteemed by a man,
1285 When a bound sword, forged by the hammer,
    The sword stained with gore, the boar on the helmet,
    Strong in its edges, opposite cleaves.
    Then was in the hall the hard-edged drawn,
    The sword o'er the seats, many a broad shield
1290 Raised firm in hand: of helmet one thought not,
    Of burnie broad, when terror him seized.
    She was in haste, would thence away,
    Her life preserve, when she was discovered.
    Quickly had she of one of the warriors
1295 Firmly laid hold, when she to fen went:
    He was to Hrothgar the dearest of men
    In the office of comrade by the two seas,
    A shield-warrior strong, whom she in rest killed,
    A hero renowned.   Not there was Beowulf,
1300 But other room before was assigned,
    After the treasure-giving, to the great Geat.
    Noise was in Heorot: she in its gore took
    The well-known hand.   Grief was renewed
    Again in the dwellings; 'twas not a good trade,
1305 That they on both sides payment should make
    With the lives of their friends. Then was the old king,
    The hoary warrior, in sorrowful mood,
    When he his chief thane, deprived of life,
    The dearest one, knew to be dead.
1310 Quickly was Beowulf brought to the hall,
    The victory-blest hero.   At dawn of day
    Went one of carls, the noble warrior,

Himself with his comrades, where the wise one
   awaited,
Whether for him the Almighty will ever,
1315 After this woe-spell, a change of things work.
Went then on the floor the man war-renowned
With his band of men (the hall-wood resounded),
Until he addressed the wise one in words,
The lord of the Ingwins, asked if to him were,
1320 As he had wished, the night undisturbed.
XXI. Hrothgar then spoke, the defence of the Scyldings :
" Ask not thou for health.   Sorrow 's renewed
To the Danes' people : dead is Aeschere,
Of Yrmenlaf the elder brother,
1325 My trusted counsellor and my adviser,
My right-hand man, when we in battle
Defended our heads, when warriors engaged,
When the boars clashed : such should an earl be,
An excellent prince, as Aeschere was.
1330 She was to him the murderer in Heorot,
The restless death-demon : I know not whither,
Proud of her prey, she frightful withdrew,
Well-known from her meal.   The feud she avenge l
For that thou yester-night Grendel didst kill
1335 In a powerful way by your hard grips,
Because he too long my own people
Lessened and killed : in battle he fell,
Of his life guilty, and now came another,
A mighty fell foe, her son would avenge,
1340 And further has laid her feud upon us ;
Wherefore it may seem to many a thane,
Who for his ring-giver mourns in his mind,
A bale hard to bear ; now lies the hand helpless,
Which used to gratify all of your wishes.
1345 I the land-dwellers, my own people,
Counsellors-in-hall, that have heard say

That they used to see a pair of such
Mickle mark-steppers holding the moors,
Spirits of elsewhere : one of these was,
1350 As they most certainly might then perceive,
A woman's form : the other one wretched
In the likeness of man his exile trod —
Except he was greater than any man else —
Whom in yore-days Grendel they named,
1355 The dwellers-on-earth : they know not their father,
Whether any to him was before born
Of wicked spirits.   They in a dark land,
Cliffs of wolves, dwell, windy nesses,
Dangerous marshes, where mountain-stream
1360 Under clouds of the nesses flows down below,
Lake under the earth.   It is not far hence
In measure by miles that the mere stands,
Over which hang the rustling groves,
Wood firm in its roots ; they cover the water.
1365 There one every night a strange wonder may see,
Fire on the flood : so wise a one lives not
Of the children of men that knows its bottom :
Although the heath-stepper pressed by the dogs,
The stag, strong in horns, may seek the grove,
1370 Pursued from afar, his life will he give,
His life on the shore, ere in it he will
Hide there his head.   That 's no unhaunted place ;
Thence the boiling of waters rises up high
Wan to the clouds, when the wind rouses
1375 The hateful storms, while dark grows the air,
The heavens weep./ Now is ready counsel
Again in thee alone.   The abode yet thou knowest not
The terrible place, where thou mayest find
The much-sinning being : seek if thou dare.
1380 I for the contest thee will repay
With old-time treasures, as I before did,

With twisted gold, if thou comest away."
XXII. Beowulf then spoke, Ecgtheow's son:
   " Sorrow not, wise man !   It is better for each
1385 That his friend he avenge than that he mourn much
   Each of us shall the end await
   Of worldly life : let him who may gain
   Honor ere death.   That is for a warrior,
   When he is dead, afterwards best.
1390 Arise, kingdom's guardian!   Let us quickly go
   To view the track of Grendel's kinsman.
   I promise it thee : he will not escape,
   Nor in earth's bosom, nor in mountain-wood,
   Nor in ocean's depths, go where he will.
1395 Throughout this day do thou patience have
   Of each of thy woes, as I ween of thee !"
   Up leaped the agéd one, thanked he then God,
   The mighty Lord, for what the man spoke.
   Then was for Hrothgar a horse provided,
1400 A steed with curled mane : the ruler wise
   Well-equipped went ; the band stepped forth
   Of bearers of shields.   The foot-tracks were
   On the forest-paths widely perceived,
   The course o'er the plain : she went straight ahead
1405 O'er the murky moor, of knightly thanes bore
   The noblest one deprived of life,
   Of those who with Hrothgar defended his home.
   Went he then over, the offspring of princes,
   The steep, stony slopes, the narrow ways,
1410 The strait single paths, the unknown course,
   The headlands steep, many houses of nickers.
   He one of few went on before,
   Of the wise men, the plain to view,
   Until he all at once the mountain-trees
1415 O'er the gray stone found bending down,
   The joyless wood : the water stood under

Gory and restless. To all the Danes 'twas,
To the friends of the Scyldings, bitter in mood,
To many a thane sorrow to suffer,
1420 To each one of earls, after of Aeschere
On the holm-cliff the head they found.
The flood boiled with blood (the people looked on),
With the hot gore. The horn at times sang
The ready war-song. All the warriors sat down ;
1425 They saw then in the water many of worm-kind,
Strange sea-dragons, seeking the sea,
Such nickers lying out on the ness-slopes,
As at mid-day often prepare
A sorrowful voyage on the sail-road,
1430 Worms and wild beasts : rushed they away
Fierce and angry ; the noise they perceived
The war-horn sound. The prince of the Geats
With his arrowed bow deprived one of life,
Of strife with the sea, so that stood in his vitals
1435 The hard war-arrow : he was in the holm
The slower in swimming, whom death took away.
Quickly was in the waves with their boar-spears,
Their hookéd swords, fiercely attacked,
Pressed after with struggles and to the ness drawn.
1440 The wonderful monster : the men looked upon
The terrible stranger. Beowulf girded him
With noble armor, not for life did he care :
The war-burnie should, woven with hands,
Wide and well-wrought, seek out the sea,
1445 That which his body could well protect,
So that him battle-grip might not in breast,
The mad one's assault, injure in life :
But the bright helmet protected his head,
Which was to mingle with the depths of the sea,
1450 Adorned with treasure seek the sea-waves,
Encircled with diadem, as in days of old

The weapon-smith wrought it, wondrously framed it,
Set with swine-bodies, so that it never after
The flaming war-swords might be able to bite.
1455 That was not then the least of strong helps,
That to him in need Hrothgar's orator lent:
Of that hilted sword Hrunting was name;
That was a chief one of old-time treasures;
Its edge was of iron, with poison-twigs stained,
1460 Hardened with battle-gore; ne'er failed it in fight
Any of men, who it wielded with hand,
He who durst tread the terrible paths,
The folk-place of foes: that was not the first time,
That deeds of valor it should perform.
1465 The kinsman of Ecglaf remembered not now,
Mighty in strength, what he before spoke
Drunken with wine, when the weapon he lent .
To a better sword-bearer; he himself durst not
Under waves' tumult venture his life,
1470 Heroic deeds work; there he lost fame,
A name for valor; not so with the other,
When he for battle himself had prepared.
XXIII. Beowulf then spoke, Ecgtheow's son:
"Bethink thyself now, great kinsman of Healfdene,
1475 Thou ruler wise, now I'm for the way ready,
Gold-friend of men, of what we once spoke,
If I in thy service should at any time
Of my life be deprived, that thou wouldst ever be
To me when gone hence, in stead of a father.
1480 Be thou a protector to my knightly thanes,
My trusty comrades, if war take me off:
Also the treasures, which thou gavest me,
Do thou, dear Hrothgar, to Hygelac send.
May then by the gold the Geat's lord perceive,
1485 Hrethel's son see, when he looks on the treasure,
That I did one find in man's virtues good,

A giver of rings, him enjoyed while I might.
And do thou let Hunferth the ancient relic,
The wonderful sword, the widely-known man
1490 The hard-edged have.   I shall with Hrunting
Fame for me gain, or death will me take."
After these words the prince of the Weder-Geats
Hastened with valor, not for an answer
Would he await.   The water-flood took
1495 The mighty warrior : then was a day's space
Ere the bottom-plain he might perceive.
Soon that discovered she who the flood's realm,
Eager for blood, for fifty years held,
Grim and greedy, that there some one of men
1500 The monster's abode sought out from above.
She grasped then against him, the warrior seized
In her terrible claws ; not sooner she injured
His body sound : the burnie him shielded,
So that she might not pierce through the corslet,
1505 The locked linkéd sark, with fiendish fingers.
Bore then the sea-wolf, when she came to the
          bottom,
The giver of rings to her own abode,
So that he might not, tho' he was brave,
His weapons wield, but him many strange ones
1510 Oppressed in the sea : many a sea-beast
With battle-tusks his war-sark brake ;
The monsters harassed him. The earl then per-
     ceived
That he in sea-hall, he knew not what, was,
Where him no water in aught might harm,
1515 Nor for the roofed hall might lay hold of him
Sudden grip of the flood : the fire-light he saw,
The brilliant beams brightly shining.
The good one perceived then the wolf of the bottom,
The mighty mere-woman ; he gave a strong stroke

1520 With his battle-bill, withheld not the blow,
    So that on her head the ringéd blade sounded
    A greedy war-song. Then the stranger perceived
    That the war-weapon would not cleave through,
    Injure her life, but the edge failed
1525 The prince in his need: before it endured
    Many hand-meetings, the helmet oft clave,
    The fated one's corslet: that was the first time
    To the dear treasure that power had failed.
    Again was determined, not lacking in prowess,
1530 Mindful of fame, the kinsman of Hygelac:
    Then threw the etched brand, with jewels adorned,
    The angry warrior, that it on the earth lay,
    Strong and steel-edged; he trusted to strength,
    The hand-grip of might: so shall a man do,
1535 When he in war thinketh to gain
    Praise everlasting, nor for his life careth.
    Seized then by the shoulder (cared she not for the
        contest)
    The War-Geats' prince Grendel's mother,
    Threw then battle-brave, for he was enraged,
1540 The life-destroyer, that she on the floor fell.
    She him again quickly the hand-grip repaid
    With her fierce claws, and seized him fast:
    Then stumbled the weary one, strongest of warriors,
    The fighter-on-foot, so that he fell.
1545 She sat on the hall-guest and drew her short sword.
    Broad and brown-edged, her son would avenge,
    Her only child. On his shoulder lay
    The braided breast-net: that his life saved,
    Against point and edge entrance withstood.
1550 Then had he perished, Ecgtheow's son,
    'Neath the broad bottom, the chief of the Geats,
    Had not the war-burnie lent help to him,
    The hard battle-net, and had not holy God

Directed the victory, the all-knowing Lord;
1555 The Ruler of heaven adjudged it aright;
Easily afterwards he again rose.
XXIV. 'Mongst the armor he saw then a victory-blessed
      weapon,
Old sword of the eotens strong in its edges,
Honor of warriors: that was choicest of weapons,
1560 But it was greater than any man else
To the war-play was able to bear,
Good and ornate, the hand-work of giants.
He seized the chained hilt, the Scyldings' champion,
Raging and battle-fierce, the ringéd sword bran-
      dished,
1565 Hopeless of life angrily struck,
So that 'gainst her neck it strongly grasped,
Broke the bone-rings; the bill pierced through
Her fated body: she on the floor fell;
The sword was bloody, in his deed he rejoiced.
1570 The blade's beam shone, the light stood within,
Just as from heaven brightly doth shine
The firmament's candle.   He looked through the hall,
Turned then by the wall, uplifted the weapon
Strong by its hilts Higelac's thane,
1575 Angry and firm: the edge was not useless
To the war-hero, but he quickly would
Grendel repay many warlike assaults
Of those which he wrought to the West-Danes
Oftener by far than for one time,
1580 When he of Hrothgar the hearth-companions
Slew in their sleep, whilst sleeping ate
Of the Danes' folk fifteen of men,
And such another bore he away,
A sorrowful prey: he paid him for that,
1585 The warrior fierce, as he in rest saw
Weary of war Grendel there lying

Of life deprived, as him before injured
The combat at Heorot.　His body sprang far,
When he after death suffered the blow,
1590 The strong sword-stroke, that struck off his head.—
Soon that perceived the cunning churls,
Those who with Hrothgar gazed on the sea,
That the waves-stirring all was commingled,
The surge stained with blood. The hoary-haired elders
1595 Concerning the good one together thus spoke,
That they for the prince looked not again,
That he, flushed with victory, would come to seek
Their mighty chief, since it seemed to so many
That the sea-wolf him had destroyed.
1600 Then came the ninth hour ; the ness forsook
The valiant Scyldings : he departed thence home,
The gold-friend of men.　The strangers sat,
Sick in their mind, and stared on the sea :
They knew and weened not, that they their dear lord
1605 Himself might see. — The sword then began
On account of the battle-gore in clots of blood
The war-bill to vanish (that was a wonder),
So that it all melted likest to ice,
When the frost's fetters the Father unlooses,
1610 The ice-rope unwinds, He who has control
Of times and tides : that is true Creator.
Took he not in the dwelling, the Weder-Geats' prince,
More of rich treasures, though he many there saw,
But only the head and the hilts together,
1615 With jewels adorned : the sword ere melted,
The etched brand burnt : the blood was so hot,
The strange-spirit poisonous, who therein died.
Soon was he swimming who lived through the strife,
The foes' fierce assault, dived he up through the
water :
1620 The stirrings of waves all were cleansed,

The regions wide, when the strange-spirit
Left his life-days and this fleeting creation.
Came then to the land the seamens' protector
Strong-minded swimming, joyed in his sea-booty,
1625 The mighty burden of what he had with him.
They went then to meet him, gave thanks to God
The brave band of thanes, rejoiced in their chief,
For that they him safe might again see.
Then from the strong one helmet and burnie
1630 Quickly was loosed : the lake became thick,
Water under the clouds stained with war-gore.
Forth went they thence on the foot-paths
Glad in their hearts, measured the land-ways,
The well-known roads ; the very bold men
1635 From the sea-cliff were bearing the head
With great exertion to each one of them :
Of the courageous four warriors should
On the spear-shaft with labor bear
To the gold-hall the head of Grendel,
1640 Until forthwith to the hall came
Fourteen brave men and fierce in war
Of the Geats going : the lord of men with them,
Brave in the crowd, trod the mead-plains.

VIII.

*Beowulf's account of the fight. Hrothgar's moralizing
speech. On the morrow Beowulf bids farewell to
Hrothgar, receives presents, and returns to his
ship.*

Then entering came the prince of the thanes,
1645 The man brave in deeds, honored in fame,
The battle-fierce warrior, Hrothgar to greet.
Then was by the hair on the floor borne

The head of Grendel, where the men drank,
Frightful to earls and the lady also,
1650 A wonderful sight: the men on it gazed.
XXV. Beowulf then spoke, Ecgtheow's son:
"Lo! we thee this sea-booty, son of Healfdene,
Prince of the Scyldings, with joy have brought
As a token of fame, which thou gazest on here.
1655 I that with my life scarcely escaped;
Under water in battle risked I the work
With great exertion; almost would have been
Ended the struggle, had not me God shielded.
I might not in battle with Hrunting the sword
1660 Aught then perform, though that weapon is good:
But the Ruler of men granted to me
That I on the wall saw beautiful hanging
An old mighty sword (often has He directed
Those without friends), that I brandished the weapon.
1665 Then I slew in the contest, when time favored me,
The house's keepers. Then did the battle-bill,
The etched brand, burn, as sprang forth the blood,
The hottest of battle-gore: I the hilt thence
Bore from my foes, avenged their ill-deeds,
1670 Death-plague of the Danes, as it was right.
I promise thee then that thou mayest in Heorot,
Sorrowless sleep with thy warrior-band,
And each of the thanes of thine own people,
Of old and of young; thou needst not for them fear,
1675 Chief of the Scyldings, from this direction
Life-bale for thy earls, as thou didst before."
Then was the golden hilt to the old warrior,
The hoary war-chief, given in hand,
The old work of giants: it went into the keeping,
1680 Since the fall of the devils, of the lord of the Danes,
The cunning smiths' work, when this world forsook
The bad-hearted being, the opposer of God,

Devoted to death, and his mother also :
It went into the power of the noblest one
1685 Of the world-kings by the two seas,
Of those who in Sceden-ig treasure divided.
Hrothgar then spoke, on the hilt looked,
The old relic on which was the origin written
Of an old contest : the flood afterwards slew,
1690 The rushing sea, the race of the giants ;
Badly they fared : that people was hostile
To the Lord eternal ; therefor a reward
Through waters' flood the Almighty them gave.
So was on the guard of purest gold
1695 In runic letters rightly engraved,
Was set and said, for whom that sword,
Choicest of weapons, first had been wrought
With wreathed hilt snake-adorned.   Then the chief
        spoke,
The son of Healfdene (kept silent all) :
1700 "Lo ! that he may say who truth and right
Works for his people, the past all remembers,
An old home-guardian, that this earl was
One born of the best.   Thy fame is wide-spread
Through distant ways, Beowulf my friend,
1705 Over each nation : with patience thou holdest it all,
Thy might with prudence of mind.   I shall to thee
        grant
My friendship, as we before spoke : thou shalt be
        for comfort,
All long-assured, to thine own people,
To heroes for help.   Not so was Heremod
1710 To the children of Ecgwela, the Honor-Scyldings ;
He throve not for their pleasure, but for their
        slaughter,
And for death-plagues to the Danes' people :
Slew he enraged his table-companions,

His chosen comrades, till he went alone,
1715 The mighty prince, from human joys:
     Though him mighty God in joy of strength.
     In power exalted, over all men
     Him had uplifted, yet in his heart grew
     A bloodthirsty feeling: he did not give rings
1720 To the Danes by right: joyless abode he,
     So that for this strife sorrow he suffered,
     Misery lasting. By that teach thou thyself,
     Practise man's virtues. This tale for thee
     Have I, old in years, told. 'Tis a wonder to say
1725 How mighty God to the race of mankind,
     Through His great mind, wisdom divides,
     Homes and nobility: He rules over all.
     Sometimes on love permits He to turn .
     The thoughts of the man of mighty race,
1730 Gives him in his home the joy of earth,
     A sheltering city of men to possess,
     Makes subject to him parts of the world,
     A kingdom wide, so that he of it may not,
     For his lack of wisdom, think of the end:
1735 He dwells in plenty, nor him does aught check,
     Sickness nor age, nor for him does sorrow
     Grow dark in his mind, nor a foe anywhere
     Show him sword-hate, but for him all the world
XXVI. Wends at his will. He knows not the worse,
1740 Until him within a portion of pride
     Waxes and grows, when sleeps the keeper,
     The guard of the soul: that sleep is too firmly
     Bound up with sorrows; very nigh is the slayer,
     Who from arrowed bow spitefully shoots.
1745 Then is he in his breast pierced under his helmet
     With a sharp arrow: he cannot defend him
     From the evil strange-orders of that cursed spirit:
     Him seems it too little what he long held;

He with evil mind covets, gives not for boasting
1750 Gold-plated rings, and he future fate
Forgets and neglects, for God gave him before,
The Ruler of glory, a share of earth's honors.
It at the end afterwards happens
That the frail body fleeting doth fail,
1755 Fated doth fall: another succeeds,
He who undisturbed treasures divides,
The earl's former store, cares not for its owner.
Guard against wrong-doing, Beowulf dear,
Best one of heroes, and choose thou the better,
1760 Counsels eternal.   Care not for pride,
Mighty warrior.   Now is thy strength's fame
Lasting a while: soon after it shall be
That sickness or sword shall rob thee of might,
Or clutch of the fire, or swell of the flood,
1765 Or grip of the sword, or flight of the arrow,
Or fearful old age, or light of the eyes
Shall fail and grow dark: it suddenly shall be
That thee, great warrior, death shall overcome.
So I the Ring-Danes a hundred half-years
1770 Ruled under heavens, and secured them by war
Against many tribes throughout this mid-earth,
With spears and with swords, so that any foe
Under circuit of heaven reckoned I not.
Lo! to me in my home a change of this came,
1775 Sorrow for joy, after Grendel became
The foe of long years, my constant home-seeker:
I from this hostility continually suffered
Much sorrow of mind.   Thanks to the Creator,
The Lord eternal, whilst in life I remained,
1780 That I on this head drenchéd with gore,
After long sorrow, look with my eyes.
Go now to thy seat, partake of feast-joy,
Thou honored in war.   To us shall be many

Of treasures in common, when morning shall come."
1785 The Geat was glad-minded, went he then soon
His seat to take, as the wise one bade.
Then was as before for the courageous
Sitters-in-hall fitly prepared
Another time.   Night's canopy lowered
1790 Dark o'er the warriors.   The band all arose;
The white-haired one his bed would seek,
The agéd Scylding.   The Geat beyond measure,
The brave shield-warrior, it pleased to rest:
Soon the hall-thane him of his way weary,
1795 The comer-from-far, forth led to his couch,
He who through courtesy all would supply
Of the wants of the thane, as at that day
The farers-by-sea were wont to have.
The great-hearted rested: the hall arose
1800 Wide and gold-decked: the guest slept within,
Until the black raven the joy of heaven
Blithe-hearted announced, when came the bright light
Shooting o'er shadows.   The warriors hastened:
The aethelings were back to their people
1805 Ready to go: he would far thence,
The high-minded guest, visit his vessel.
The brave one then bade Hrunting bear
The son of Ecglaf, bade take his sword,
Precious weapon, thanked him for the loan,
1810 Said that he counted the war-friend good,
Mighty in battle, not in words blamed he
The edge of the sword: that was a brave man.
When for their march ready, in armor equipped,
The warriors were, went by the Danes honored
1815 The prince to the throne, where was the other,
The battle-brave man: Hrothgar he greeted.
XXVII. Beowulf spoke, Ecgtheow's son:
   "Now we sea-goers desire to say,

Comers-from-far, that we intend
1820 Hygelac to seek: we were here well
Supplied in our wishes: thou served'st us well.
If I then on earth may in any manner
More of thy heart's love gain for myself,
Ruler of men, than I have yet done,
1825 For works of war I soon shall be ready.
If I that learn o'er the flood's course,
That thee thy neighbors with dread oppress,
As hating thee they sometimes have done,
To thee I shall bring thousands of thanes,
1830 Of heroes for help. Of Hygelac I know,
Lord of the Geats, though he be young
Chief of his folk, that he me will aid
By words and by deeds that I may thee honor,
And to thee for help my spear-shaft bear,
1835 The power of my might, if thou needest men.
If Hrethric then at the courts of the Geats,
The king's son, aid seeks, he may there many
Of his friends find: far countries will be
Better sought for by him who is worthy."
1840 Hrothgar then spoke to him in answer:
"These words to thee the all-wise Lord
Sent into thy mind: ne'er heard I more wisely
In so youthful age any man speak:
Thou art in might strong and in mind old,
1845 A counsellor wise. I count on the hope,
If this may happen that the spear take,
Terrible battle, the son of Hrethel,
Sickness or weapon, thine own chieftain,
People's shepherd, and thou hast thy life,
1850 That the Sea-Geats will not have a better,
To choose as their king, any one, than thee,
Hoard-keeper of heroes, if thou wilt hold
Thy kinsmen's kingdom. Me thy bold courage

Long pleases so well, Beowulf dear.
1855 Thou hast now caused that to these nations shall,
To the Geats' people and to the Spear-Danes,
Peace be in common and strife shall cease,
The hostile contests which they ere suffered:
There shall be, whilst I wield the wide realm,
1860 Treasures in common; many another
With presents shall greet o'er the swan's bath:
The ringéd ship shall o'er the sea bring
Presents and love-tokens. I know that the people
Towards foe and towards friend are firmly disposed,
1865 In everything blameless after old custom."
Then still to him the defence of earls gave,
The son of Healfdene, twelve jewels besides,
Bade him with these presents his own dear people
Seek in good health and quickly return.
1870 Kissed him then the king noble in birth,
The prince of the Scyldings kissed the best thane,
And round the neck clasped; tears from him fell,
The gray-haired one: he had hope of both,
The agéd man, more of the latter,
1875 That they might again each other see,
Courageous in council. The man was so dear
That he the breast-flood could not restrain,
But in his breast, fast in his mind's fetters,
For the dear man a secret longing
1880 Burned through his blood. — Beowulf thence,
The gold-adorned warrior, the grassy plain trod,
Proud of his treasure: the sea-goer awaited
Its own possessor, which at anchor rode.
Then was on the way the gift of Hrothgar
1885 Often extolled: that was a king
In everything blameless, till old age removed him
From his might's joys, which has oft oppressed many

IX.

Beowulf's arrival at home and welcome by Hygelac. The
episode of Offa and Thrytho. Beowulf's account of
his journey. Freaware and Ingeld. Presents of
Beowulf and Hygelac.

XXVIII. Came then to the sea the very brave ones,
    The band of attendants ; their burnies they bore,
1890 Their locked body-sarks. The land-guard perceived
    The return of the earls, as he before did :
    He did not with harm from the cliff's head
    Greet then the guests, but towards them rode,
    Quoth that as welcome the Weders' people,
1895 The mail-clad warriors, went to their ship.
    Then was on the shore the spacious boat,
    The ring-prowed ship, with battle-weeds laden,
    With horses and jewels ; the mast arose
    Over Hrothgar's hoard of treasures.
1900 He to the boat-guard, bound with gold-work,
    A sword then gave, so that after he was
    On the mead-bench from the jewel more honored,
    The costly heir-loom. He went in his sea-boat
    To stir the deep water, the Danes' land forsook.
1905 Then was to the mast one of sea-cloths,
    Sail by rope fastened. The vessel groaned ;
    Not there the sea-floater did the wind o'er the waves
    In its course hinder : the sea-goer went,
    The foamy-necked floated forth o'er the water,
1910 The curvéd-prowed went o'er the sea-waves,
    Until the Geats' cliffs they might descry,
    The well-known nesses. The keel pressed up,
    Urged by the wind it stood on the land.
    Quickly was at the sea the harbor-guard ready,
1915 Who long time before for the dear men

Longing had gazed afar on the ocean :
He to the shore fastened the wide-bosomed ship
With anchor-chains fast, lest the waves' force
The winsome boat might carry away.
1920 He bade then bear up the nobles' treasures,
Jewels and beaten gold ; not for them far thence
Was it to seek the giver of rings :
Hygelac, Hrethel's son, there at home dwelt,
Himself with his comrades near the sea-wall.
1925 The building was fine, the prince a good king,
High was the hall, Hygd very young,
Wise, well-instructed, although winters few
Under the city-locks she may have dwelt,
The daughter of Haereth : she was not, though, nig-
    gardly,
1930 Nor sparing in gifts, to the Geats' people,
In costly jewels.   Modthrytho committed,
The great folk-queen, horrible crime :
No brave one durst that undertake,
Of dear companions, except her liege lord,
1935 That on her by day he should look with his eyes :
But he wrought for himself death-fetters firm,
Twisted by hand : quickly afterwards was,
After the hand-grip, the sword appointed,
So that the carved weapon must it decide,
1940 Tell the death-bale.   Such is not queenly custom
For a woman to practise, though she be peerless,
That a peace-weaver of life should deprive,
On account of fierce anger, any dear man.
That indeed checked the kinsman of Heming.
1945 The drinkers of ale other word said,
That she of folk-woes less did inflict,
Of hostile deeds, after she first was
Gold-adorned given to the young warrior,
The brave young noble, after she Offa's hall,

1950 O'er the dark flood, by her father's command,
     Sought in her journey, where she afterwards well,
     On royal throne, by gifts renowned,
     Her portion of life whilst living enjoyed,
     Held her great love for the prince of heroes,
1955 Of all mankind, as I have heard say,
     The very best one by the two seas,
     Of human race: for that Offa was
     By gifts and war-deeds, the very brave man,
     Widely renowned; with wisdom he ruled
1960 His own possessions: thence Eomor sprang
     For help to heroes, the kinsman of Heming,
     Grandson of Garmund, crafty in contests. —
XXIX. Went then the brave with his trusty band
     Himself o'er the sand the sea-beach treading,
1965 The wide-stretching shores: the world-candle shone,
     Sun inclined from the south. They kept on their
          journey,
     Went in their might, till the earls' defence,
     The slayer of Ongentheow within in the city,
     The good young war-king they then heard say
1970 Rings was dividing. To Hygelac was
     The journey of Beowulf quickly made known,
     That there in the palace the warriors' defence,
     His shield-companion, living was come,   .
     Hale from the battle-play to the court going.
1975 Quick was prepared, as the mighty one bade,
     For the foot-guests the hall within.
     Sat he then opposite, who 'scaped from the strife,
     Kinsman with kinsman, after his lord
     With courtly speech the loyal one greeted,
1980 With mighty words. With mead-cups went
     Through the high hall the daughter of Haereth;
     The people she served, the ale-cups she bore
     To the men at hand. Hygelac began

His comrade-in-arms in the high hall
1985 Kindly to ask (wish to know urged him),
What were the journeys of the Sea-Geats:
" How befell on your way, Beowulf dear,
When thou so suddenly thoughtest afar
The strife to seek o'er the salt water,
1990 Battle at Heorot?   But didst thou for Hrothgar
The widely-known woe in aught remove,
For the great chief?   I for that in distress,
In sorrow-waves pined: the journey I trusted not
Of the dear man.   Thee long I begged
1995 That thou the death-spirit by no means wouldst seek,
Wouldst let the South-Danes themselves put an end to
Their war against Grendel.   I give thanks to God,
For that I may see thee now safe and sound."
Beowulf spoke, Ecgtheow's son:
2000 " That is now plain, Hygelac lord,
Our great struggle, to many of men,
What a war-time of Grendel and me
Was in the place where he very many
Sorrows had wrought to the Victor-Scyldings,
2005 Misery perpetual: all that I avenged,
So no kinsman of Grendel need now rejoice
At the morning-sound over the earth,
He who shall live longest of that evil race,
By danger surrounded!   At first I came there
2010 To the ringed hall Hrothgar to greet:
Soon for me the great son of Healfdene,
After he knew of my intention,
Near his own son a seat provided.
The crowd was in joy; ne'er saw I my life long
2015 Under heaven's vault of sitters-in-hall
Greater mead-joy!   Sometimes the great queen,
Peace-bringer of nations, went through all the hall,
Urged the young sons: oft she a bracelet

Gave to a warrior, ere she went to her seat.
2020 Sometimes 'fore the court the daughter of Hrothgar
To the earls at the end the ale-cup bore,
Whom I Freaware the sitters-in-hall
Heard call by name, where she buckled treasure
Gave to the heroes.   She had been promised,
2025 Young, gold-adorned, to Froda's glad son :
Therefore it has happened to the friend of the Scyl-
        dings,
The kingdom's ruler, and he counts that a gain,
That he with the woman a part of fierce feuds,
Of quarrels appeased.   Often the courtiers,
2030 After folk's fall, in a little while
The deadly spear takes, though good be the bride.
XXX. It may therefore displease the prince of the Heath-
        obards,
And each of the thanes of these peoples,
When he with the woman goes into the hall,
2035 That a son of the Danes on her should attend :
For on him there shines the bequest of the agéd,
Hard and ring-decked, the Heathobards' treasure,
While they with weapons were able to rule,
Until they misled to the shield-play
2040 Their dear companions and their own lives.
Then speaks at the beer-drinking he who sees the
        jewel,
An old spear-warrior, who all remembers,
Spear-death of men (fierce is his mind),
Begins, sad in mood, of the young warrior
2045 The spirit to rouse by thoughts in his mind,
War-bale to excite, and this word speaks :
' Mayst thou, my friend, know now the sword,
Which thine own father bore into battle
Under his helmet for the last time,
2050 The precious weapon, where the Danes slew him,

The battle-place held, when dead lay Withergyld,
After heroes' fall, the Scyldings brave?
Now here a son of some one of these murderers,
In his weapons rejoicing, goes into the hall,
2055 Boasts of the murder and bears the jewel,
Which thou with right shouldest possess.'
So he advises and each time reminds
With bitter words, until the time comes
That the woman's thane, for the deeds of his father,
2060 After the sword's stroke blood-stained sleeps,
Guilty of his life : thence will the other
Warrior escape ; he knows the land well.
Then are there broken on either side
The sword-oaths of earls, after in Ingeld
2065 Are roused deadly feuds, and in him woman's love
After care-waves cooler becomes.
Therefore I count not on the faith of the Heatho-
            bards,
Folk-peace sincere, kept with the Danes,
Friendship confirmed. — I shall speak forth
2070 Yet about Grendel, that thou mayst well know,
Giver of treasure, what was the result
Of the hand-fight of men.   After heaven's gem
Glided over the earth, the angry fiend came,
The terrible even-guest, to make us a visit,
2075 Where we unharmed guarded the hall.
There was Hondscio destined for fight,
Life-bale to the fated : he lay the first,
The belted warrior : to him was Grendel,
To the great war-thane, a mouth-destroyer,
2080 The dear man's body all he swallowed.
Not sooner out then yet empty-handed,
The bloody-toothed murderer mindful of woes
From the gold-hall was willing to go,
But he, strong in might, made trial of me,

2085 With ready hand grasped me. His glove was hang-
     ing,
    Wide and wonderful, in cunning bands fast;
    It was all wrought with curious skill
    With devil's craft and dragon's skins;
    He me therein, guiltless of crime,
2090 The fierce deed-doer, wished to destroy,
    One of many: it might not be so,
    After in anger upright I stood.
    Too long is to tell how I the folk's foe
    For each of his ills a hand-reward paid,
2095 Where I, my prince, thine own people
    Honored by deeds. Away he escaped,
    A little while life's joys enjoyed:
    Yet of him a trace remained behind,
    His right hand in Heorot, and he humbled thence,
2100 Sorrowing in mind, to the sea-bottom sank.
    Me for this contest the friend of the Scyldings
    With plated gold much rewarded,
    With many treasures, when morning came,
    And we at the banquet had seated ourselves.
2105 There was song and glee: the agéd Scylding,
    Who much had heard, of past times related;
    Sometimes the warrior the joy of the harp,
    The play-wood touched; sometimes sang a song
    True and sorrowful; sometimes a strange tale
2110 Truthfully told the wide-hearted king;
    Sometimes then began, burdened with age,
    The hoary warrior to tell of his youth's
    Prowess in battle; his breast swelled within,
    When he old in years their number remembered.
2115 So we therein the live-long day
.   Partook of hall-joys, until night came on,
    Another to men. Then was again quickly
    Ready for vengeance the mother of Grendel,

She sorrowful went: death took off her son,
2120 War-hate of the Weders. The wondrous woman
Her son avenged, a warrior killed
Courageously; there was from Aeschere,
The agéd counsellor, life departed.
Nor might they him, when morning came,
2125 Delivered to death, the folk of the Danes
With fire consume, and on the pyre place
The dearly-loved man; the body she bore
In the fiend's embrace 'neath the mountain-stream.
That was to Hrothgar the greatest of sorrows,
2130 Of those that long the prince befell.
Then the chief me by thine own life
Adjured, sad in mind, that I in the sea's flood
Should do valiant deeds, should risk my life,
Should honor gain; he promised reward.
2135 I then of the water, which is widely known,
The grim and fearful guard of the deep found.
There a while was to us a hand-to-hand fight;
The sea welled with gore, and I of the head robbed
In the ground-hall the mother of Grendel
2140 With a strong sword; I scarcely from thence
My life bore away; not yet was I fated;
But the earl's defence to me after gave
Many of treasures, the son of Healfdene.
XXXI. So the folk-king lived as was right:
2145 Not at all had I lost by these rewards,
This meed of might, but he gave me treasures,
The son of Healfdene, at mine own will,
Which I will to thee, warlike king, bring,
Willingly offer. Still on thee is all
2150 Of favor dependent: I have very few
Of near relations save, Hygelac, thee."
He bade then bring in the boar's-head-sign,
The battle-high helmet, the hoary burnie,

The war-sword ornate, his word then uttered :
2155 "This cuirass to me Hrothgar then gave,
     The crafty chief, bade with some words
     That I of its origin first should thee tell,
     Said that it had Iiorogar king,
     Prince of the Scyldings, for a long while :
2160 Not to his son sooner would he it give,
     To the brave Heoroweard, though to him he were
          dear,
     The defence of the breast.   Use thou it well!"
     I heard that to the armor four horses too,
     Exactly alike, in their tracks followed,
2165 Yellow as apples : he to him gave possession
     Of horses and jewels.   So shall a friend do,
     Not at all cunning snares weave for another,
     With secret craft death for him prepare,
     His hand-companion.   To Hygelac was,
2170 In battle brave, his nephew devoted,
     And each to the other mindful of kindness.
     I heard that the necklace he to Hygd gave,
     The curious treasure which Wealhtheow gave him,
     The prince's daughter, three horses likewise,
2175 Slender and saddle-bright : to her after was,
     After the ring-giving, the breast adorned.
     So bravely bore him Ecgtheow's son,
     The man famed in wars, by his good deeds,
     He did after right, not at all slew the drunken
2180 Hearth-companions : his mind was not cruel,
     But he of mankind with greatest power,
     The mighty gift, which God him gave,
     The warlike one kept.   Long he was despised,
     As him the Geats' children did not reckon good,
2185 Nor him at the mead-bench as worthy of much
     The lord of the people would then esteem ;
     They weened very strongly that he was slothful,

An unwarlike prince ; a change after came
To the glory-blessed man of each of his sorrows.
2190 The earl's defence bade then bring in,
The warlike king, Hrethel's bequest
Adorned with gold : there was not 'mong the Geats
A better treasure in the shape of a sword :
That did he place in Beowulf's keeping,
2195 And to him gave seven thousand of gold,
A house and dominion.   To them both together
Among the people was inherited land,
A home and its rights, more to the other,
A wide-spread kingdom, to him who was better.

———◆◆———

BEOWULF AND THE DRAGON.

X.

Beowulf is king.   The dragon's hoard robbed.   The fiery
vengeance of the dragon.

2200 That happened after in later days
By battle-contests, when Hygelac died,
And to Heardred swords of battle
Under the shields were as a murderer,
When him there sought 'mong his victor-people
2205 The warriors bold, the Battle-Scylfings,
By war oppressed the nephew of Hereric.
After to Beowulf the kingdom broad
Came into hand : he held it well
Fifty winters (then was the king agéd
2210 The home-keeper old) until one began
On the dark nights, a dragon, to rule,
Who on the high heath a treasure protected,
A steep stony mountain : the path under lay,
To men unknown.   There within went

2215 Some one of men, who took his desire
From the heathen hoard : a certain hand-vessel,
Adorned with gold, he there then took,
Made of red gold, so that was robbed
By the fire sleeping the treasure's guardian
2220 By a thief's craft : the prince after learnt,
The innocent warrior, that he was enraged.
XXXII. Not at all of free-will the dragon-hoard's heap
Sought he of himself, who him sorely injured,
But through necessity the thane of some one
2225 Of the children of men hateful blows fled,
Through dire compulsion, and therein entered
The innocent man.   Soon it was at that time
That there to the stranger dread terror stood :
Yet miserable he there within took,
2230 The frightened soul who terror suffered,
A costly-wrought vessel.   There were many of such
In the earth-cave, of ancient treasures,
As them in old days some one of men,
The great bequest of a noble race,
2235 With thoughtful mind there had concealed,
The precious treasures.   Death them all took away
In former times, and the only one still
Of the people's nobles who there longest lived,
The friend-mourning guardian, wished that to delay,
2240 So that he a short time longer the treasures
Might there enjoy.   A mountain all ready
Stood on the plain near to the waters,
Steep by the ness, firm, inaccessible :
There within bore of noble treasures
2245 The keeper of rings a part hard to carry
Of beaten gold, banning words spoke :
"Keep thou now, earth, since men may not,
The possession of earls.   Lo ! before it in thee
Good men obtained : war-death took away,

2250 Fearful life-bale, each one of men,
     Of mine own people, who gave up this life:
     They saw hall-joy. I've not one to bear sword,
     Or care for the cup of beaten gold,
     The dear drinking-vessel: the chiefs elsewhere are
          gone.
2255 The hard helmet shall, with gold adorned,
     Be deprived of its jewels: the polishers sleep,
     Those who the battle-mask should ever brighten;
     And likewise the breast-plate, which in battle endured
     O'er clash of shields the blows of weapons,
2260 Crumbles after the warrior: nor may the ringed
          burnie
     After the battle-chief go far and wide
     By the side of heroes: there 's no harp's joy,
     Play of the glee-wood, nor does the good hawk
     Through the hall fly, nor the swift horse
2265 The city-courts paw. Mighty death has
     Many of mortals sent on their way."
     So sad in mind in sorrow mourned
     One over all, miserable lived he
     By day and night, until death's wave
2270 Touched him at heart. The precious hoard found
     The old twilight-foe open standing,
     He who burning the mountains seeks,
     The naked dragon, who flies by night
     Surrounded by fire: him the earth-dwellers
2275 Saw from afar. He shall inhabit
     The hedge on the earth, where he heathen gold
     Guards old in years: he shall not be the better.
     So the folk-foe three hundred winters
     Held in the earth one of hoard-halls
2280 Wondrously great, until him one angered,
     A man, in his mind: he bore to his lord
     The jewelled cup, a peace-offering gave

To his own lord. Then was the hoard found,
Hoard of rings borne away; the prayer was granted
2285 To the miserable man : his lord beheld
Men's ancient work for the first time.
When the dragon awoke, strife was renewed:
He went 'round o'er the stone, the brave-minded
    found
His enemy's foot-track : he forth had stepped
2290 With secret craft near the head of the dragon.
So may one not fated easily escape
  Woes and exile, who the Almighty's
Favor possesses. The hoard-keeper sought
O'er the ground eagerly, would find the man,
2295 Who to him in sleep this harm had done :
Hot and fierce-minded oft he went 'round the cave
Now all without: there was not any man
On the heath's waste. Yet in battle he joyed,
In hostile deeds : he returned to the mountain,
2300 The precious cup sought : he that soon found,
That some one of men the gold had discovered,
The costly treasures. The hoard-keeper waited,
Angry in mind, until evening came :
Was then enraged the guard of the mountain,
2305 Would many people with fire repay
For the dear drinking-cup. Then was the day gone
At the will of the dragon, nor in the cave longer
Would he abide, but with flame went he forth,
With fire provided. The beginning was fearful
2310 To the folk in the land, as it too quickly
On their ring-giver sorely was ended.
XXXIII. Then the demon began to vomit with fire,
To burn the bright dwellings : the flame-light stood
For terror to men : not there aught living
2315 The hateful air-flyer was willing to leave.
The worm's war-power widely was seen,

The hostile one's hate both near and far,
How the war-foe the folk of the Geats
Hated and harmed : to his hoard then he hastened,
2320 The secret rich hall, before the day-time.
He had the land-dwellers with fire o'erwhelmed,
With flame and burning : to his mountain he trusted,
His war-might and wall : that hope him deceived.

XI.

*Beowulf prepares for the contest. The deaths of Hygelac
and of Heardred recalled. Beowulf's reminiscences.
The death of Herebeald and Hrethel's sorrow. Beowulf's slaying of Daeghrefn. Beowulf seeks the
dragon alone. The fiery fight. Wiglaf goes to his
help. The wounding of Beowulf. The death of the
dragon. Wiglaf brings out the treasure. Beowulf's
death.*

Then was to Beowulf the terror made known
2325 Quickly in truth, that of his own
The best of houses in fire-waves melted,
The gift-seat of the Geats. That was to the good
one
Distress in mind, greatest of sorrows.
The wise one weened that he the Almighty
2330 Against the old laws, the eternal Lord,
Had grievously angered : his breast within swelled
With gloomy thoughts, as to him was not usual.
The fire-drake had the people's fastness,
The island without, the landed possessions,
2335 With fire destroyed : for him then the war-king,
The Weders' prince, revenge devised.
Bade then work for him the warriors' defence,
The lord of earls, all made of iron

A wonderful war-shield : he knew very well
2340 That forest-wood him could not help,
The shield against fire.   He of his fleeting days,
Excellent prince, the end should await
Of his worldly life, and the worm likewise,
Although his hoard-treasure he long had held.
2345 Scorn did he then, the prince of rings,
That he the wide-flier with host should seek,
With a large army : he feared not the contest,
Nor did he for aught count the serpent's war-might,
His strength and prowess, for that he before many
2350 Conflicts survived, though dangers encountering,
Clashings of battle, since he of Hrothgar,
A victory-blessed hero, the hall had cleansed,
And in battle destroyed the kinsmen of Grendel,
The hateful race.   That was not the least
2355 Of hand-encounters, where one Hygelac slew,
When the Geats' king in the contests of war,
Friendly lord of the folk, in the land of the Frisians,
The son of Hrethel, in sword-blood died,
Struck down with the brand.   Thence Beowulf came
2360 By his own might, swam through the sea :
He had on his arm thirty and one
Of battle-equipments, when he in the sea went.
The Hetwaras did not need to be boastful
Of their foot-contest, who against him before
2365 Were bearing their shields : few again came
From the war-hero to visit their home.
Ecgtheow's son swam o'er the sea's surface,
Unhappy alone back to his people,
Where to him Hygd offered treasure and kingdom,
2370 Rings and king's throne : she the child trusted not,
That 'gainst other peoples the nation's seats
He knew how to hold, when Hygelac was dead.
Not sooner might the forsaken ones find

At the hands of the prince in any respect,
2375 That he to Heardred would be a lord,
Or he the kingdom was willing to choose :
Yet he him 'mong the people with friendly lore held,
Kindly with honor, until he was older,
And the Wedergeats ruled. Him did the banished
     ones
2380 Seek o'er the sea, Ohthere's sons ;
They had 'gainst the lord of the Scylfings rebelled,
The most excellent one of the sea-kings,
Who in the Swedes' kingdom treasure divided,
A mighty prince. That to him was life's end :
2385 He there at the banquet the death-wound received
With blows of the sword, Hygelac's son,
And then he departed, Ongentheow's son,
To visit his home, when Heardred lay dead,
Let Beowulf hold the royal throne,
2390 And rule the Geats : that was a good king !
XXXIV. He remembered reward for that people's loss
In later days ; to Eadgils he was,
To the helpless a friend, with an army supported
O'er the wide sea Ohthere's son,
2395 With war-might and weapons : he after avenged him
For the cold care-journeys, of life the king robbed. —
So he had survived each one of struggles,
Of dangerous contests, Ecgtheow's son,
Of mighty deeds, till that very day
2400 That he 'gainst the serpent was going to fight.
He went one of twelve, swollen with rage,
The prince of the Geats, the dragon to view ;
He had then learnt whence rose the feud,
Deadly hate to his warriors : into his keeping came
2405 The great treasure-cup through the hand of the
     finder.
He was in the band the thirteenth man,

Who the beginning of this contest caused,
Sad in mind, fettered, despised he should thence
Point out the plain : he against his will went
2410 For that he knew the earth-hall alone,
Cave under the earth near the sea-waves,
Near the rushing of waters, which was within full
Of jewels and wire-work : the monstrous guard,
The ready warrior, the gold-treasures held,
2415 Old under the earth : that was no easy purchase
To be obtained for any of men.
Sat then on the ness the warlike king
Whilst farewell he bade to his hearth-companions,
The gold-friend of the Geats : his mind was sad,
2420 Restless and death-ready, Weird very nigh,
Which should approach the agéd man,
Seek the soul's hoard, asunder divide
The life from the body ; not then was long
The life of the prince in flesh enclosed.
2425 Beowulf spoke, Ecgtheow's son :
" Many war-struggles in youth I survived,
Times of battle ; I remember all that.
I was seven winters, when me lord of treasures,
Dear ruler of peoples, took from my father ;
2430 Supported and kept me Hrethel the king,
Gave me treasure and feast, remembered our kin
    ship ;
I was never to him at all a more hateful
Man in his palace than one of his sons,
Herebeald and Haethcyn or Hygelac mine.
2435 There was for the eldest contrary to right
By the deeds of his kinsman a death-bed prepared,
Since him did Haethcyn from his hornéd bow,
His own dear lord, with arrow pierce,
Missed he the mark and his kinsman did shoot,
2440 One brother the other, with bloody dart :

That was fee-less fight, wickedly sinned,
Sorrow-bringing to breast; should yet, however,
The lord unavenged from life depart.
So is it sorrowful to an agéd churl
2445 To live to see that his son hang
Young on the gallows: then he utters a moan,
A sorrowful song, when his son hangs
For joy to the raven, and he him may not help,
Old and experienced, aught for him do.
2450 Always is remembered on each one of mornings
His son's departure; he cares not another
To hope to see born in his own palace,
An heir to his throne, when this one has,
Through might of death, suffered such deeds.
2455 He sorrowful sees in his son's dwelling
The wine-hall empty, the windy rest-place
Of merriment robbed; the warrior sleeps,
The prince in his grave; no sound of harp's there,
No sport in the courts, as there were once.
2460 XXXV. Then he goes to his chamber, sings sorrow-
        ful songs,
The one for the other: too empty all seemed,
Fields and dwelling. So the Weders' defence
For Herebeald sorrow of heart
Welling up bore: he might not at all
2465 Upon that murderer the feud avenge;
Not sooner might he wreak his hate on the warrior
With evil deeds, though he was not to him dear.
He then with this sorrow, which befell him so sore,
Gave up human joy, God's light did choose,
2470 Left to his sons, as a wealthy man does,
Land and chief city, when from life he departed.
Then was feud and strife of the Swedes and the
        Geats,
O'er the wide water contest in common,

A hard battle-struggle, after Hrethel was dead,
2475 Whilst to them were Ongentheow's sons
Bold and warlike, friendship would not
O'er the sea keep, but around Hreosna-mount
Terrible inroads often did make.
For that mine own kinsmen vengeance did take,
2480 For the feud and the wrong, as it was known,
Although the other it bought with his life,
A heavy price: to Haethcyn was,
To the Geats' lord, the war destructive.
Then heard I that on th' morrow one kinsman the
      other
2485 With edge of the sword avenged on the murderer,
When Ongentheow Eofor sought out:
The war-helmet split, the agéd Scylfing
Fell down sword-pale; his hand remembered
Of strife enough, the death-blow withheld not. —
2490 I to him the treasures which he me gave
Repaid in war, as it was given me,
With the shining sword; he gave to me land,
A dwelling and home. There was not to him lack,
That he 'mong the Gifths, or 'mong the Spear-Danes,
2495 Or in the Swedes' kingdom, needed to seek
A warrior worse, him buy with a price:
I always would go before him on foot,
Alone in front, and so for life shall I
Enmity work, while this sword permits,
2500 Which often stood by me early and late.
Then 'fore the courtiers was I to Daeghrefn
For a hand-slayer, the Hugs' brave warrior:
Not he the jewels to the king of the Frisians,
The breast-adornment, was able to bring,
2505 But in battle he fell, the standard's keeper,
The prince in his might; sword was not his slayer,
But for him battle-grip the swellings of heart,

The bone-house broke. Now shall the bill's edge,
Hand and hard sword, fight for the hoard."
2510 Beowulf said, with boastful words spoke
For the last time : " I survived many
Wars in my youth ; yet now I will,
Old people's guard, the contest seek,
With honor work, if me the fell foe
2515 From his earth-hall dare to seek out."
Greeted he then each one of men,
The brave helmet-bearers, for the last time,
His own dear comrades : " I would not the sword
      bear,
Weapon 'gainst worm, if I knew how
2520 Upon this monster I might otherwise
My boast maintain, as once upon Grendel.
But I there expect hot battle-fire,
Breath and poison : therefore I have on me
Shield and burnie.   I will not the hill's guard,
2525 The foe, flee from even part of one foot,
But at wall it shall be as for us Weird provides,
Each man's Creator : I am in mind brave,
So that 'gainst the war-flier from boast I refrain.
Await ye on mountain, clad in your burnies,
2530 Heroes in armor, which one may better,
After the contest, from wounds escape
Of both of us.   That is not your work,
Nor the might of a man but of me alone,
That he 'gainst the monster his strength should try,
2535 Heroic deeds do.   I shall with might
The gold obtain, or war shall take off,
Terrible life-bale, your own sovereign."
Arose then by the rock the warrior fierce
Brave under his helmet, his battle-sark bore
2540 'Neath the stone-cliffs, to the strength trusted
Of one man alone ; such is no coward's work.

He saw then by the wall (he who very many,
In man's virtues good, of contests survived,
Struggles of battle, when warriors contended)
2545 A stony arch stand, a stream out thence
Break from the mountain; the burn's flood was
With battle-fire hot; might not near the hoard
One without burning any while then
Endure the deep for the flame of the dragon.
2550 Let then from his breast, since he was enraged,
The Wedergeats' prince his words go forth,
The strong-hearted stormed: his voice came in,
In battle clear-sounding, 'neath the hoar stone.
Strife was stirred up; the hoard-keeper knew
2555 The voice of a man: there was not more time
Friendship to seek. First there came forth
The breath of the monster out of the rock,
Hot battle-sweat; the earth resounded.
The man 'neath the mountain his shield upraised
2560 'Gainst the terrible demon, the lord of the Geats:
Then was the ring-bowed eager in heart
The contest to seek. The sword ere brandished
The good war-king, the ancient relic
Sharp in its edges: to each one was
2565 Of those bent on bale dread from the other.
The strong-minded stood against the steep rock,
The prince of friends, when the worm bent
Quickly together: he in armor awaited.
Went he then burning advancing in curves,
2570 To his fate hasting; the shield well protected
In life and in body a lesser while
The mighty chief than his wish sought,
If he that time, on the first day,
Was to control, as Weird did not permit him
2575 Triumph in battle. His hand he uplifted,
The prince of the Geats, the fearful foe struck

With the mighty relic, so that the edge softened
Brown on the bone, bit less strongly
Than the folk-king need of it had,
2580 Oppressed with the fight. Then was the hill's keeper,
After the battle-blow, fierce in his mood,
Threw with death-fire; far and wide spread
The flame of the battle. Of triumphs he boasted not,
The gold-friend of the Geats: the war-bill failed
2585 Naked in fight, as it should not,
Excellent weapon. That was no easy task,
So that the mighty kinsman of Ecgtheow
The plain of this earth was to forsake,
Must at the worm's will take up his abode
2590 Elsewhere than here; so shall every man
His fleeting life leave. It was not then long
That the fierce ones again each other met.
The hoard-keeper raged, his breast swelled with
breath:
A second time he suffered distress
2595 Surrounded by fire, who before ruled his folk.
Not at all in a band did his companions,
Children of nobles, him stand around
With warlike virtues, but they to wood went,
Protected their lives. In one of them welled
2600 His mind with sorrows; friendship may never
Be at all put aside by one who thinks well.
XXXVI. Wiglaf was named Weohstan's son,
The worthy warrior, prince of the Scylfings,
Kinsman of Aelfhere. He saw his lord
2605 Under his helmet the heat endure;
He remembered the favor, that he once to him gave
The rich dwelling-place of the Waegmundings,
Each one of folk-rights which his father possessed.
He might not then refrain, his hand seized the shield,
2610 The yellow wood, he drew his old sword:

That was among men Eanmund's bequest,
Ohthere's son, to whom in strife was,
To the friendless exile, Weohstan the slayer
By the edge of the sword, and he bore to his kins-
    men
2615 The brown-colored helmet, the ringéd burnie,
The old giant's sword that Onela gave him,
His own relation's war-equipments,
Ready war-weapons: he spoke not of the feud,
Though he had slain his brother's son.
2620 He the ornaments held many half-years,
Bill and burnie, until his son might
Heroic deeds work, as his old father:
He gave to him then war-weeds 'mong the Geats,
Countless number of each, when he from life went
2625 Old on his last journey. Then was the first time
To the young warrior that in storm of war
With his dear lord he should engage;
His courage failed not, nor his kinsman's bequest
Softened in battle: that the dragon perceived,
2630 After they two together had gone.
Wiglaf then spoke many suitable words,
Said to his comrades (sad was his mind):
"I remember that time when we received mead,
When we did promise to our dear lord
2635 In the beer-hall, who gave us these rings,
That we for the war-weeds him would repay,
If to him such need ever should happen,
For helmets and hard swords, since in host he us
    chose
For this expedition of his own will,
2640 Thought of honors for us, and gave me these treas-
    ures,
Us whom he deemed spear-warriors good,
Brave helmet-bearers, although our lord

This noble work intended alone
To accomplish for us, ward of his folk,
2645 Because he of men most noble deeds did,
Rashly-bold actions.   Now is the day come
That our own chieftain has need of the strength
Of warriors good : let us to him go,
Help the war-prince whilst there is heat,
2650 Fierce fiery terror.   God knows in me,
That to me 'tis far dearer that my own body
With my gold-giver the flame should embrace.
Not becoming, methinks, is't that we should bear
        shields
Again to our home, unless we may sooner
2655 Strike down the foe, the life protect
Of the Weders' chief.   I know it well,
That he does not deserve that he alone shall
Of the Geats' nobles sorrow endure,
Fall in the battle : now shall sword and helmet,
2660 Burnie and battle-dress, to us both be common."
Went he then through the flame, his war-helmet bore
For help to his lord, spoke a few words :
" Beowulf dear ! do thou all well,
As thou in thy youth long ago said'st,
2665 That thou would'st not let for thyself living
Honor e'er cease ; now shalt thou, strong in deeds,
Firm-minded prince, with all thy might
Thy life protect ; I shall assist thee."
After these words the angry worm came,
2670 The terrible demon, a second time
With fire-waves shining to seek his foes,
The hostile men.   With flame-billows burned
The shield to the rim : the burnie might not
To the young spear-warrior assistance afford.
2675 But the young hero 'neath the shield of his kinsman
With courage went, when his own was

Destroyed by flames.   Then still the war-king
Was mindful of fame, of his mighty strength,
Struck with his war-bill, that it stood in the head
2680 Forcibly driven : broke in two Naegling,
Failed in battle Beowulf's sword,
Old and gray-etched. 'T was not granted to him,
That him of the sword the edges were able
To help in the battle : that hand was too strong,
2685 Which any of swords, by my hearsay,
With its stroke tested, when to battle he bore
The sharp-wounding weapon : 't was not for him
better.
Then was the folk-foe for the third time,
The bold fire-dragon, mindful of feuds,
2690 Rushed on the strong one, since space him allowed,
Hot and war-fierce, clasped around all the neck
With his sharp bones : he was all bloodied
With the life-blood ; gore welled in waves.
XXXVII. Then I heard say in the folk-king's need
2695 The earl displayed unceasing bravery,
Strength and valor, as was natural to him :
He cared not for his head, but the hand burned
Of the brave man, where he helped with his strength,
So that the fell demon he struck somewhat lower,
2700 The hero in armor, that the sword sank in,
Shining and gold-plated, that the fire began
After to lessen.   Then still the king
His senses possessed, struck with his war-knife,
Cutting and battle-sharp, which he bore on his
burnie :
2705 The Weders' defence cut the serpent in two.
The foe they felled, force drove out life,
And they him then both had destroyed,
Kindred princes : such should a man be,
A thane in need.   That was to the prince

2710 The last of his victories by his own deeds,
  Of work in the world. Then 'gan the wound,
  Which on him the earth-drake before had inflicted,
  To burn and to swell: that soon he perceived
  That in his breast deadly ill welled,
2715 Poison within. Then the prince went,
  So that he by the rock, wise in his mind,
  Sat on his seat, on the giants' work looked,
  How the stone-arches, fast on their columns,
  The earth-hall eternal held there within.
2720 Then with his hands him bloody with gore,
  The mighty prince, the excellent thane
  His own dear lord with water laved,
  Weary of battle, and his helmet unloosed.
  Beowulf said: he spoke of his wound,
2725 His deadly-pale wound (he knew very well
  That he had spent his time allotted
  Of the joy of earth; then was all gone
  Of his days' number, death very nigh):
  "Now I to my son would wish to give
2730 These war-weeds of mine, if to me was granted
  Any inheritor hereafter to be
  The heir of my body. This people I ruled
  Fifty of winters; there was not a folk-king,
  Of those dwelling around any at all,
2735 Who me durst meet with his war-friends,
  With terror oppress. I awaited at home
  The appointed time, kept mine own well,
  Sought not hostilities, nor for myself swore
  Many oaths falsely; I for all that,
2740 With deadly wounds sick, now joy may have;
  Hence the ruler of men need not to me charge
  The murder of kinsmen, when shall depart
  My life from my body. Now do thou quickly go
  To see the hoard 'neath the hoar stone,

2745 Wiglaf my dear one, now the serpent lies dead,
　　　 Sleeps sorely wounded, robbed of his treasure.
　　　 Be now in haste that I the old riches,
　　　 The treasure may view, thoroughly scan
　　　 The bright precious gems, that I may the easier,
2750 On account of the treasure, give up mine own
　　　 Life and my people that I long held."
XXXVIII. Then heard I that quickly Weohstan's son,
　　　 After these words, his wounded lord
　　　 Sick from battle obeyed, bore his ringed net,
2755 His battle-sark woven, 'neath the roof of the mountain.
　　　 Saw then victorious. when he by the seat went,
　　　 The brave kin-thane many of treasures,
　　　 Glittering gold on the ground lying,
　　　 Wonder on wall and the den of the worm,
2760 The old air-flier, drinking-cups standing,
　　　 Vessels of old-time wanting the polisher,
　　　 Deprived of their ornaments.　There was many a
　　　　　 helmet
　　　 Old and rusty, many arm-bracelets
　　　 Curiously twisted.　The treasure may easily,
2765 The gold in the ground, each hoard of mankind
　　　 In value exceed, let him hide it who will.
　　　 Likewise he saw standing an all-golden banner
　　　 High over the hoard, greatest of wonders,
　　　 Wrought with hand-craft; from it light stood,
2770 So that the ground-plain he might perceive,
　　　 Examine the treasures.　There was not of the serpent
　　　 Any appearance, but sword took him off.
　　　 Then I heard say, in the cave the hoard robbed,
　　　 The old work of giants, one man alone,
2775 Bore on his bosom the cups and the plates
　　　 At his own will; the banner he took,
　　　 Brightest of beacons, a bill sheathed with brass
　　　 (Its edge was of iron) of the old lord,

Who of these treasures was the protector
2780 For a long while, bore fiery terror
Hot, deadly-rolling, on account of the hoard
In the midst of the night, till he in death perished.
In haste was the messenger for return ready,
Provided with treasures; wonder him moved,
2785 Whether he the high-minded alive would find
In that grassy spot, the prince of the Weders,
Deprived of strength, where he him before left.
He then with the treasures the mighty prince,
His own dear lord, bleeding did find
2790 At the end of his life.   He began him again
With water to sprinkle, until the word's point
Brake through his breast-hoard: Beowulf spoke,
The old man in sorrow (the gold he viewed):
" I for these treasures to the Lord of all thanks,
2795 To the glorious King, in words do speak,
To the Lord eternal, — which I here look upon,
For this that I might for mine own people
Before my death-day such treasures obtain.
Now I for the hoard of jewels have paid
2800 Mine own agéd life; do ye now supply
The needs of my people; I may not longer be here.
Bid ye the war-famed a mound to make
Bright after the pyre at the sea's point,
Which shall for remembrance to mine own people
2805 Raise itself high on the Whale's ness,
That it the sea-farers hereafter may call
Beowulf's mound, who shall their high ships
O'er the sea's mists from afar drive."
He put from his neck the golden ring,
2810 The bold-minded prince, gave to the thane,
The young spear-warrior, his gold-adorned helm,
Collar and burnie, bade him use them well:
" Thou art the last left of our own kindred

Of tho Waegmundings.   Weird carried away all
2815 Of mine own kinsmen at the time appointed,
Earls in their strength: I shall go after them."
That was to the agéd the very last word
In his breast-thoughts, ere the pyre he chose,
The hot fiery waves: from his breast went
2820 His soul to seek the doom of the saints.

XII.

Wiglaf rebuke$ the thanes.   Speech of the messenger.   The
death of Haethcyn, pursuit of Hygelac, and death
of Ongentheow.   The warriors arrive.   Wiglaf's
speech.   They enter the cave.   The funeral-pyre.
Beowulf's mound.

XXXIX. Then it had happened to the young man,
With sorrow of mind, that he on the earth saw
The dearest one at the end of his life
Livid become.   The slayer too lay,
2825 The fearful earth-drake, of life bereft,
Oppressed with bale: the ring-treasures longer
The twisted serpent might not control,
But the swords' edges took him away,
The hard battle-notched leavings of hammers,
2830 So that the wide-flier, still from his wounds,
Fell on the earth nigh the hoard-hall;
Not at all through the air did he go springing
In the midst of the night, proud of his treasures
Showed he his form: but he to earth fell
2835 On account of the handwork of this battle-prince.
Now that in the land to few of men throve
Of might-possessors, as I have heard say,
Though he were bold in every deed,

That one should meet the poison-foe's breath,
2840 Or the ring-hall disturb with his hands,
If he were to find the waking guard
On the mount watching. By Beowulf was
The portion of treasures paid for with death:
It had for each the end obtained
2845 Of fleeting life. — 'Twas not then long after
That the cowardly ones the wood forsook,
The unwarlike truth-breakers, ten together,
Who durst not before fight with their spears
In their liege lord's very great need:
2850 But they ashamed bore then their shields,
Their weeds of war, where the agéd one lay;
They gazed upon Wiglaf. He wearied sat,
The fighter-on-foot, near his lord's shoulders,
Refreshed him with water: it naught him availed.
2855 He might not on earth, though he well would,
In the great prince his life retain,
Nor the Almighty's will could he change;
The doom of God in deeds would dispose
For each one of men, as He now doth.
2860 Then was from the youth an answer grim
For him easy gotten, who before lost his valor.
Wiglaf then spoke, Weohstan's son,
The sorrowful man (he looked on the unloved):
" Lo ! that may he say who will speak truth,
2865 That the folk-king who gave you the treasures,
The war-equipments, in which ye there stand,
When he on the ale-bench often presented
To the hall-sitters helmet and burnie,
The prince to his thanes, such as anywhere bravest
2870 From far or nigh he was able to find, —
That he without doubt the weeds of war
To no purpose wasted. When war him assailed,
Not at all did the folk-king of his comrades-in-war

Have cause to boast: yet God him granted,
2875 The Ruler of victory, that himself he avenged
    Alone with his sword, when he had need of strength.
    I to him little life-defence might
    In battle afford, and yet I undertook
    Beyond my power my kinsman to help:
2880 He was always the worse, when I with the sword
        struck
    The life-destroyer: the fire ran stronger,
    Welled from his breast. Too few defenders
    Pressed round the prince, when the evil befell him.
    Now taking of jewels and giving of swords,
2885 All joy of home for your own kindred,
    Comfort shall cease: of rights of land
    Each one of men of this kindred tribe
    Must be deprived, after the princes
    From afar hear of your desertion,
2890 Inglorious deed. Death shall be better
    To each one of earls than a life of disgrace."
XL. He bade then the battle-work tell at the hedge
    Upon the steep cliff, where the earl-band
    The morning-long day sad in mind sat,
2895 The warriors with shields, in expectance of both,
    The final day and the return
    Of the dear man. Little kept silent
    Of the new tidings he who rode o'er the ness,
    But he in truth spoke on all sides:
2900 "Now is the joy-giver of the folk of the Weders,
    The lord of the Geats, fast in his death-bed,
    Fills his grave-rest by the deeds of the worm.
    Along side of him lies the life-winner too
    Dead from knife's wounds; with sword might he not
2905 Upon the monster in any way
    A wound inflict. Wiglaf sits there,
    Sits over Beowulf Weohstan's son,

The earl o'er the other of life deprived,
With care attentive, keeps the death-watch
2910 Of friend and of foe.   Now the people expect
A time of strife, after well-known
To the Franks and the Frisians the fall of the king
Becomes far and wide.   The contest was made
Strong 'gainst the Hugs, when Higelac came
2915 With his ship-army going to the land of the Frisians,
Where the Hetwaras felled him in battle,
Bravely him conquered with their over-might,
So that the mailed-warrior was forced to bow,
Fell midst his warriors ; no ornaments gave
2920 The prince to his nobles.   To us ever after
The Merwings' friendship was not to be granted.
Nor do I from the Swedes peace or good faith
At all expect ; but it was widely known
That Ongentheow of life deprived
2925 Haethcyn, Hrethel's son, near Ravens' wood,
When through their pride at first did seek
The warlike Scylfings the folk of the Geats.
Soon to him the agéd father of Ohthere,
Old and terrible, gave a hand-stroke,
2930 Hewed down the sea-chief, rescued his wife,
The old man his spouse, robbed of her gold,
The mother of Onela and of Ohthere,
And then he followed his deadly foes
Until they went in great distress
2935 Into Ravens' wood, deprived of their lord.
Then besieged he with host those left by the sword,
Weary with wounds, woes oft he promised
To the miserable band the livelong night :
Said, he in the morning with the edge of the sword
2940 Them would destroy, some on gallows hang
For sport to the fowls.   Comfort afterwards came
To them sad in mind along with daylight,

After they Hygelac's horn and trumpets'
Sounding perceived, when the brave one came
2945 In the track going of his peoples' earls.
XLI. There was bloody track of Swedes and of Geats,
The slaughter of men widely observed,
How the folk fought the feud one with another.
The good one then went with his companions,
2950 The agéd most sad, the fastness to seek,
The earl Ongentheow betook himself higher;
He had of Hygelac's prowess heard tell,
The proud one's war-craft; in resistance he trusted
    not,
That he the sea-men might then withstand,
2955 His hoard protect from the sea-farers,
His children and wife; he went after thence
Old 'neath the earth-wall.   Then was given pursuit
To the folk of the Swedes, their banner to Hygelac.
Forth then they went o'er the Peace-plain,
2960 After the Hrethlings pressed into the hedge;
There Ongentheow was, with the edge of the sword,
The gray-haired one, forced to remain,
So that the folk-king had to submit
To Eofor's sole will; angrily him
2965 Wulf, son of Wonred, attacked with his weapon,
So that for the blow blood spurted in streams
Forth under his hair.   He was not though afraid,
The agéd Scylfing, but quickly repaid
In a worse way that fatal blow,
2970 After the folk-king thither turned round:
Might not then the quick son of Wonred
To the old churl a hand-stroke give,
But he on his head his helmet first cleft,
So that, stained with blood, he had to bow,
2975 Fell on the earth: he was not yet fated,
But he himself raised, though the wound pained him.

Then the brave thane of Hygelac let
With his broad sword, when his brother lay down,
The old sword of giants, the helmet of giants
2980 Break over the shield-rim: then bowed the king,
The herd of the folk; he was struck to his life.
Then were there many who bound up his brother,
Quickly him lifted, when for them it was settled
That they the battle-place were to possess,
2985 Whilst one warrior the other robbed,
From Ongentheow took his burnie of iron,
His hard hilted sword and his helmet besides,
The hoary one's armor to Hygelac bore.
The armor he took and to them fairly promised
2990 Gifts to his people, and kept his word too.
The lord of the Geats paid for the contest,
The son of Hrethel, when he came to his home,
To Eofor and Wulf with very rich jewels,
To each of them gave a hundred thousand
2995 Of land and locked rings (for the gifts him need not
       reproach
Any man on mid-earth, since they heroic deeds
       wrought),
And then to Eofor gave his sole daughter,
The home-adornment, as a pledge of his favor.
That is the feud and that the enmity,
3000 Hate deadly of men, wherefore I expect
That the Swedes' people against us will seek,
After they learn that our own lord
Is 'reft of his life, him who before held
Against his foes his hoard and kingdom
3005 After heroes' fall, the Scylfings brave,
Wrought his folk's good and further still
Heroic deeds did. — Now is haste best
That we the folk-king there should behold,
And him should bring who gave us rings

3010 To the funeral-pyre. There shall not a part only
       With the brave perish, but there's hoard of treasure,
       Gold without number, bitterly purchased,
       And now at the last with his own life
       Rings has he bought: these fire shall devour,
3015 The flame consume; no earl shall wear
       A jewel in memory, nor the beautiful maid
       Have on her neck a ring-adornment,
       But she shall sad in mind, robbed of her gold,
       Often not once tread a strange land,
3020 Now that the war-chief laughter has left,
       Mirth and enjoyment. For this shall the spear be,
       Many a one morning-cold, clasped with the fingers,
       Held in the hands; not at all shall harp's sound
       Wake up the warriors, but the wan raven,
3025 Eager over the fated, often shall speak,
       Say to the eagle how he joyed in the eating,
       When with the wolf he robbed the slain."
       So the brave warrior then was telling
       Some tales of evil: he did not speak falsely
3030 His facts nor words. — The band all arose;
       Sadly they went 'neath the Eagles' ness,
       With flowing tears, the wonder to see.
       Then they found on the sand deprived of his life,
       Holding his resting-place, him who rings them gave
3035 In former times: then was the last day
       Past to the good one, so that the war-king,
       The prince of the Weders, a wondrous death died.
       First there they saw a stranger being,
       The worm on the plain opposite there,
3040 The loathsome one lying; the fiery dragon,
       The terror grim, was scorched with flames;
       He was fifty feet, in his full measure,
       Long as he lay; the air he enjoyed
       Sometimes at night, down again went

3045 To visit his den : he was then fast in death,
    He had enjoyed the last of earth-caves.
    By him there stood pitchers and cups,
    Plates too lay there and precious swords,
    Rusty and eaten-through, as in the earth's bosom
3050 A thousand of winters there they had remained,
    Since that bequest exceedingly great,
    The gold of the ancients, was bewitched with a spell,
    So that the ringed hall might one not touch,
    Any of men, unless God himself,
3055 True King of victories, to whom He would granted
    To open the hoard, the charge of enchanters,
    Even so to such man, as seemed to Him right.
XLII. Then was it seen that the way did not prosper
    To him who with wrong had hid within
3060 The hoard 'neath the wall.   The keeper ere slew
    Some one of his foes : then was the feud
    With battle avenged.   Is it a wonder
    When a warlike earl the end approaches
    Of his life-fate, when may no longer
3065 A man with his kinsmen a mead-hall in-dwell?
    So was it to Beowulf, when he the mount's keeper,
    The contest sought : he himself knew not
    How his world-severing was to take place ;
    How it against doom's-day deeply had cursed
3070 The mighty princes who that put there,
    That *that* man should be guilty of sins,
    Shut up in cursed places, fast in hell-bonds,
    Punished with plagues, who should that plain tread
    He was not gold-greedy ; he rather would have
3075 The owner's favor sooner looked on. —
    Wiglaf then spoke, Weohstan's son :
    " Oft many an earl for the sake of one
    Sorrow shall suffer, as is happened to us.
    We might not give to our dear prince,

3080 The kingdom's ruler, any advice,
      So that he might not that gold-keeper meet,
      Might let him remain where he long was,
      Dwell in his haunts until the world's end,
      Fulfil his high fate.   The hoard is looked on,
3085 Bitterly gotten: that fate was too mighty
      Which that folk-king thither enticed.
      I was therein and looked through it all,
      The treasures of hall, when 'twas allowed me,
      Not at all friendly a journey permitted
3090 In 'neath the earth-wall.   In haste I took
      A great mighty burden with my own hands
      Of the hoard-treasures, bore them out hither
      To mine own king: he was then still alive,
      Wise and still conscious: very much spoke
3095 The agéd in sorrow and ordered to greet you,
      Bade that ye should, for your friend's deeds, make
      On the place of the pyre the lofty mound,
      Mickle and mighty, as he of men was
      The most worthy warrior through the wide earth,
3100 While he city-treasures still could enjoy.
      Let us now hasten a second time
      To see and to seek that heap of treasures,
      Wonder 'neath wall.   I shall direct you,
      That ye may once more see now enough
3105 Of rings and broad gold.   Be the bier ready,
      Quickly prepared, when we come out,
      And then let us bear our own dear lord,
      The man beloved, where he shall long
      In the Almighty's keeping patiently wait."
3110 Bade he then order, Weohstan's son,
      The warrior brave, to many of men,
      Of dwellers in houses, that they the fire-wood
      Should bear from afar, the lords of the people,
      To where lay the good one: " Now shall fire eat

3115 (The wan flame shall grow) the chief of warriors,
    Him who oft awaited the iron-shower,
    When the storm of arrows, loosed from the strings,
    Leaped over the shield-wall, the shaft did its duty,
    Fitted with feathers followed the barb."
3120 Now then the wise son of Weohstan
    Called from the crowd of the king's thanes
    Seven together, the choicest ones,
    Went one of eight 'neath the hostile roof;
    One warrior brave in his hands bore
3125 A lighted torch, who went in front.
    It was not then allotted who should plunder that
       hoard,
    After unguarded any portion of it
    The warriors saw remain in the hall,
    Lie wasting away: little one sorrowed,
3130 That they hastily carried without
    The precious treasures. The dragon they shoved,
    The worm, o'er the wall-cliff, let the waves take,
    The flood embrace, the keeper of jewels.
    There was twisted gold on a wain laden,
3135 Of each countless heap: the prince was borne,
    The hoary warrior, to the Whale's ness.
XLIII. For him then prepared the folk of the Geats
    A funeral-pyre on the earth firm,
    Hung with helmets, with shields of war,
3140 With burnies bright, as he had begged.
    Laid they then in the midst the mighty prince,
    The mourning warriors their lord beloved.
    'Gan they then on the mountain the greatest of pyres
    The warriors to kindle: the wood-smoke arose
3145 From the burning pile black, the crackling flame
    Mingled with mourning (the wind-roar was still),
    Until it had broken the house of bone,
    Hot in the breast. Sad in their minds

With sorrow they mourned their dear lord's death;
3150 Also a sad song uttered the spouse,
Pained in her breast, grieved in her heart,
Mournful she frequently fettered her mind,
So that for her husband's most grievous blows
She wept, the grim fate of his bloody death,
3155 .   .   .   .   .   terror of fire
.   .   .   heaven swallowed the smoke.
Wrought they there then the folk of the Weders
A mound on the steep, which high was and broad,
For the sea-goers to see from afar,
3160 And they built up within ten days,
The warlike one's beacon; the brightest of flames
They girt with a wall, as it most worthily
Very wise men might there devise.
They in the mound placed rings and bright jewels
3165 All such precious things as before in the hoard
Brave-minded men had taken away.
They let the earth hold the treasure of earls,
Gold in the ground, where it still lives
As useless to men as it before was.
3170 Then 'round the mound the battle-brave rode,
Children of nobles (they were twelve in all),
Their sorrow would tell, grieve for their king,
Their mourning utter, and about the man speak;
His earlship they praised, and his noble deeds
3175 They extolled to the courtiers, as it is right
That one his dear lord in word should praise,
With soul him love, when he shall forth
From his own body be severed by death.
So then lamented the folk of the Geats
3180 The fall of their lord, the hearth-companions,
Said that he was a mighty king,
Mildest to men and most tender-hearted,
To his folk most kind and fondest of praise.

THE FIGHT AT FINNSBURG.

(See Beowulf 1068 et seqq., and Glossary, s. v. Finn.)

. . . .

"Brighter pinnacles never shall burn."
Then spoke the young and warlike king:
"This is not day dawning, nor flies here the dragon,
Nor here do this hall's pinnacles burn,
5 But here forth bear the deadly foes
Their ready equipments, the birds do sing,
The gray burnie clinks, the war-wood rattles,
Shield answers shaft.   Now shines this moon,
Full moon 'neath the clouds: now arise sad deeds,
10 Which will arouse this feud of a folk,
But awake ye now, warriors mine,
Have ye your hands, think upon valor,
Go on in front, be ye courageous,
Mine own heroes."   Then arose many a
15 Gold-laden thane, him girt with his sword:
Then to doors went the lordly warriors,
Sigeferth and Eaha, their swords drew forth,
And at other doors Ordlaf and Guthlaf,
And Hengest himself went in their tracks.
20 Then still Garulf Guthhere admonished,
That they noble life for the first time
To this hall's doors should not bear in armor,
Now it the battle-brave might take away:
But he inquired o'er all unconcealed,
25 The valiant warrior who the door held:
"Sigeferth is my name: I am the Secgs' chief,
A widely-known exile.   Many woes I endured,
Battles severe.   That is yet here determined,

Which of you two wilt thyself seek for me."

30 Then was on the wall the sound of slaughters;
The curved board should, in the hands of the brave
The bone-helm burst: the house-floor resounded,
Until in this fight Garulf fell down,
First one of all of these earth-dwellers,

35 Son of Guthlaf, about him many good ones,
Corpses of warriors. Wandered the raven,
Black and dark-colored: the sword-light stood,
As if all Finnsburg were set on fire.
Ne'er heard I more worthily in contest of men

40 Sixty brave heroes bear themselves better,
Never did youths sweet mead better pay for
Than to Hnaef paid his serving-men.
Bravely they fought for five of days,
Likewise of nights, as no one of them fell,

45 Of the lord's men, but they the doors held.
Then went the wounded man on his way going,
Said that his burnie was broken in two, ·
Brave in his war-dress, and his helm too was pierced
Then him soon asked the herd of the folk,

50 How had the warriors their wounds survived,
Or which of these youths　　•　　•　　•

NOTES.

CHIEFLY TRANSLATIONS OF HEYNE'S VARIATIONS FROM GREIN
IN THE TEXT OF HIS FOURTH EDITION, 1879.

Abbreviations : E. = Ettmüller. G. = Grein. G.¹ = Grein in *Bibliothek*.
G.ˢ = Grein's Ms. Gdtvg. = Grundtvig. H. = Heyne. W. = Wülcker.
Z. = Zupitza. (1) and (2) = first and second half-line.

6 (1) "The earl sorrow suffered." H.

15 (2) . . . "while they were princeless." H. W.

21 (2) . . . "'mong his father's friends." II. W.

33 (1) Literally "icy." Acc. to H., "bronze-clad."

34 (1) "Then did they lay." H. "People" added by G. W. as H.

49 (1) "Gave him to the sea;" H. W.

51 (2) . . . "the decree of fate." H. W. as G. Z. as H.

62 E. suggests *Eádgilses* for *Onġenþeówes;* Gdtvg. and Bugge
take *Elan* as part of *Onelan*, which does great violence to
the Ms. reading. See H.'s note, and cf. Holder, p. 2, l. 15.
Why not supply *æror* or *ærest* instead of a proper name?
Cf. 3169, 616, 2654. (See Additional Notes.)

73 (1) *folc-scare* = properly "division of a folk," but here probably "the public land." See Arnold's note.

82 (1) "High and wide-gabled." H.

84 (2) II. adopts Bugge's conjecture *áðum-swerian* = "to son-
and father-in-law," i.e., Ingeld and Hrothgar, which suits
the Ms.; *s* in *secg* may have been repeated from *se*. H. puts
period after 85. W. and G.ˢ as H.

131 (1) "He suffered great grief." H.

140 (1) i.e., of the fortified castle.

149 (2) . . . "therefore was it afterwards." H. W.

163 (2) . . . "to and fro wander." H.

169 (2) . . . "nor His love did he know," H., taking *his* as referring to *metode*, the Creator, rather than to *gif-stól*, the
throne; cf. H.'s note. G.ˢ as H.

171 (2) . . . "Very often he sat." H.

173 (1) " What for the bold-minded." H.

176 (1) H., who has changed his former view, says, " *nom. pl.*";
but it must be *acc. pl.*, as G.

186 (1) " By no means make a change." H.

223-4 (2) . . . " Then was the sea sailed o'er,
(1) (Ship) at end of the sea." H. See H.'s note. If *eoletes*
= sea, then " ship" must be supplied to make sense. G.'s
text gives . . . " Then was the sea-voyage
Of their course at its end." Thorpe reads *sund-lida* =
" sea-sailer." H. follows Kemble. Neither H. nor G.
make anything satisfactory out of *eoletes*. G.[3] and W. as H.

240 (2) . . . " Have borne your helmets." H. Prof. March suggests *Hrôðgâr sêcean* = " Hrothgar to seek," which suits
well; cf. 268, 339; as would also *Hrôðgâr grêtan* = " Hrothgar to greet"; cf. 1646, 2010. Ms. shows no lacuna.

247 (1) *maga* = " men," G.; *mâga* = " kinsmen," H.

249 (2) . . . " that is no common man." H. See his note.

253 (1) " As visitors free." H.

288 (2) . . . or, " knowledge possess."

299 (1) " To such a warrior." H.

302 (1) At the rope rested. H.

303 (2) H. reads *sciônon*, and takes as *praet. pl.* of a reduplicating
verb, *scânan* = " to shine."

314 H. puts (;) after first half-line, and no point at end of line.

367 " With thy converse in turn to make them glad, Hrothgar." H.

389-90 Text defective, hence these half-lines added by editors,
though Ms. shows no lacuna.

398 (2) i.e., the result of the interview; *geþing* = " fate."

403 (2) This half-line added by editors, though Ms. shows no
lacuna.

404 (2) . . . or, " before the throne stood." G.

420 (2) . . . " where I five of them bound." H.

446 (1) " A head-guard provide." H., after Simrock. Cf. H.'s
note.

461 (2) . . . " when the kin of the Weders." H., after Gdtvg.

489-90 (2) . . . " tell thy thoughts to the heroes,
(1) Thy presage of victory." H., after Müllenhoff. Cf.
H.'s note.

548 (1) " Boisterous opposed us." H.

586-7 H. thinks two half-lines omitted here, and so numbers. G.
inserts *fela* = " much" in 2d half-line.

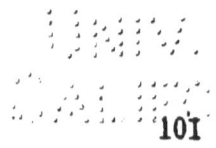
599 (2) . . . "but he in joy fighteth." H.

601 (2) omit "I," and 603 (1) omit "in." H.

611 (2) Lit., "the noise resounded." H.

647ᵃ and 647ᵇ inserted by G. H. omits both lines, and in 648 inserts *ne* before *meahton*, hence translate, "After that they sun-light might *not* see," and takes *oðð̄e*, 649, = "and," after Bugge. Cf. H.'s note. G.⁸ and W. as H.

652 (1) "Greeted in speeches." H.

668 (2) i.e., "offered himself for watch against the eoten." G.; " offered to the eoten a watcher." H.

678 (2) i.e., than Grendel counts himself.

681 (1) G. takes *gôda* = "advantages in battle"; H. = "art of fighting as a warrior." Cf. H.'s note. Why may it not mean the arms themselves?

719 (1) "A bolder warrior," H., but G. plural, which suits better.

729 (1) "A friendly band sleeping." H. Cf. 387.

736 (2) . . . "Great sorrow saw." H. Cf. 131.

741 (2) . . . "him tore unawares." H.

755 (1) i.e., he thought his hour had come.

769 (1) "For earls ale-terror." H. Lit. "ale-robbery." So W.

780 (1) i.e., "with ornaments of bone-work," or "with the stag's antlers." H.

783 (1) "Startling enough." H.

801 (2) H. inserts *þœt*. W. as G., but (:) after "soul."

804 i.e., by magical spells had made himself invulnerable.

811 (2) H. inserts *wœs*, and reads as parenthesis.

827 (1) H. puts period at end of this half-line.

836 (1) H. puts mark of parenthesis) after "Grendel." So W.

849 (1) "With hot gore boiled." H.

850 (1) "The doomed-to-death hid himself." H.

875 (1) G. reads *Sigemundes*, but Ms. *Sigemunde*. W. as G.

900, 902 H. puts (,) after 900 and (.) after 902 (1). On *Eotenum*, 902 (2), see Glossary, s.v. *Jutes*, and note.

915 (2) . . . "him," i.e., Heremod; "he," 913, i.e., Beowulf.

1031 "Bosses wire-wound were keeping without." H. W.

1033 (1) "In fight hardened." H. G., after Rieger.

1069 "The hero of Healfdene, Hnaef the Scylding." H., who begins the episode of Finn with this line.

1070 (1) The name illegible in Ms. Cf. Holder, p. 25, l. 16. W., Z.

1118 (2) . . . "the warrior arose." H., who puts period. So W.

1124 (2) . . . "gone was their strength." H., i.e.. the men themselves.

1129 (1) "All united." H., who inserts *ealles;* see his note. Cf. 1097.

1143–4 "When Hunlafing, the battle-sword,
     Best of weapons, he placed on his breast." H., who refers to Rieger. See Glossary.

1162–68 Measure varied on account of the long lines of the poem here, in 1705-7, and in 2095-6.

1224 (1) "The windy walls." H. "The windy earth-walls." W.

1226 (2) ... "Be thou to my son." H. W.

1257 (1) H. puts (,) here, and (;) after 1258 (1). So W.

1267 (1) "Sword-accursed, hated." H.

1278 (2) ... "her son's death to avenge." H.

1287 (2) ... "cleaves when they meet." H.; *andweard =* "present."

1291 (2) ... "whom terror seized." H.

1320 (1) i.e., as Beowulf had courteously bid him "Good-night."

1338 (1) i.e., having forfeited his life.

1392 (2) ... Grendel's mother is referred to as either masculine or feminine. Cf. 1260 et al.

1454 (1) "Fire nor war-swords." H. See H.'s Glossary, s.v. *brand.*

1486 (2) ... "pre-eminently good." H.

1508 (2) ... "he had courage for that." H., as parenthesis.

1583 (1) i.e., another such number, fifteen more.

1634 (2) ... "the kingly-bold men." H., as Ms.

1637 (1) H. puts (:) after this half-line, and no point after 1636.

1649 H. puts (:) at end and no point in 1650; hence = "The wonderful sight the warriors gazed on." So W.

1691 (1) "Rashly they acted." H.

1705 (2) ... "with firmness thou holdest it all." H. Cf. 1162-68.

1723–69. This moralizing speech of Hrothgar's is considered by some an interpolation. It is all omitted by E. except 1758-9, which follow 1722.

1724 i.e., about Heremod, from whose conduct the moral is drawn.

1728 (1) "Sometimes on possessions." H. G. has no word *lufa* = "landed property." It suits the sense much better than *lufe* = "love."

1731 (1) "A royal city." H.

1747 (1) *wôm,* adj., G.; *wom,* n., H.; hence, "From evil by th' strange-orders."

1757 (2) ... "cares not for terror." H.

1802-3 (2) . . . "Then came the bright sun
(1) Gliding over the ground;" H. Ms. shows no lacuna, but some words needed. Cf. Holder, p. 41, l. 23. W. as H.

1870 (1) G. inserts *cûðlíce* = "kindly," but without Ms. authority.

1873 (2) i.e., of his return, and of seeing him again. Cf. 1869.

1880-1 (2) . . . "secretly longeth
(1) The hero 'gainst blood." H., i.e., for one not related by blood to him.

1895 (1) "The shining visitors." H.

1925-6 (2) . . . "the king strong-in-might,
(1) High in the hall." H.

1931-2 (2) . . . "Thrytho showed pride,
The great folk-queen, wrought terrible deeds." H.
Thrytho seems better than Modthrytho for the name of Offa's queen. See Glossary and H.'s note. *Môd* and þrýðo separated in Ms.

1936 (1) "But she laid upon him." H.

1939 (1) "So that hostile sword." H. With *moste* begins the second hand in the Ms.

1944 (1) G., *on hôh snôd.* H., *onhôhsnode*, but with same meaning. No *e* in Ms.

1945 (2) . . . "said one to another." H. Cf. 870.

1981 (1) G. inserts *heâ* = "high." W. omits it.

2009 (1) "By fen surrounded." H.

2021 (1) i.e., at the end of the seats, the noblest warriors. H.

2029-31 (2) . . . "Often not seldom
. . . .
(1) The deadly spear rests." H., who inserts *nô* in 2029.

2030 (1) "After prince's fall." H., i.e., after the death of Froda, king of the Heathobards. Cf. 2391.

2035 i.e., that a noble Dane should protect his queen, Freaware.

2035 (2) . . . "the nobles should serve:" H.

2051 (2) . . . "when recompense failed." H., who does not take *Wíðergyld* as proper name, and includes in parenthesis 2051 (2) and 2052 (1).

2062 (1) "Escape alive." H. W. as G. Z. as H.

2069 This digression about Ingeld, put into Beowulf's mouth, reads as an anachronism.

2076 (1) *Hondscíô* now recognized by G. and H. as proper name, though not so regarded in their translations. H. takes it as dative, but *híld* = "battle," as nom.: "There was to Hondscio battle destructive."

2131 (2) . . . "by thy consent." H.

2147 (2) . . . "at his own will." H.

2152 (2) H. puts (,) after *eafor* = "boar."

2170 (1) Properly, first-cousin.

2187 (1) "They said very often." H.

2195 i.e., *sceattas*. A *sceat*, according to Bosworth, was ¼ of a *pening* and ¹⁄₆₀ of a *scylling*: perhaps = between one and two cents.

2199 (2) i.e., to Hygelac, the reigning king.

2200 (1) i.e., the possession of the kingdom, repeated in 2207. An unskilful joining of the story of Grendel to that of the dragon.

2201 (1) "To the fierce warriors." H., i.e., the Geats. Cf. 2351.

2216-31 Ms. much injured in this passage. Translation according to G.'s emendations, which, however, will not all suit the Ms.

2220-21 "The prince," i.e., Beowulf: "he," i.e., the dragon.

2224 (2) H. reads þeów = "slave," instead of þegn = "thane," which would suit well, but Holder gives þegn plainly in Ms. Other emendations of H. will not suit Holder's reprint of the Ms.

2228 (1) "The stranger," i.e., the fugitive who took refuge in the dragon's cave.

2246 (2) . . . "a few words spoke." H.　G. has *fec-word* = "banning words," and refers to H., but suggests *feá worda* = "few words." H., however, adopts *feá worda* in his 4th edition, although Holder gives *fec worda* as Ms. reading. So Z.

2253 (1) "Or bring the cup." H. W.

2268 (2) . . . "miserable wept he." H. W.

2276 (1) "Cave under the earth," H., which is better. Ms. corrupt. W. as H.

2288 (1) "He snuffed o'er the stone." H.

2297-8 (2) . . . "not there any man
　　　　(1) Was on this waste." H., which suits Ms. better.

2330 (1) i.e., the ten commandments. H.

2351 (1) "The warrior bold." H. Cf. 2201.

2361 (2) H. omits "and one," and places (. . .). Holder shows no lacuna. In 3d ed. H. gives emendations of Gdtvg., G., and Rieger, and in 4th ed. that of Bugge.

2391 (2) . . . "for that prince's fall." H., i.e., Heardred. Cf. 2030.

2393 (1) " To the helpless a foe. With an army he went." H.
See Glossary and H.'s note. Müllenhoff and Bugge support
G. Holder gives *freónd* plainly. So does Z.

2395-6 " he," i.e., Eadgils; " the king," i.e., Onela.
(2) . . . " he after avenged it
(1) With cold care-journeys." H.; " he," i.e., Beowulf;
" the king," i.e., Eadgils, the " care-journeys " being Beowulf's expedition against Eadgils.

2475 H. takes oðöe = " and," after Bugge; cf. 649. On this line
cf. also note to 2930-32.

2490 (1) i.e., to Hrethel, mentioned above, 2474 and 2430.

2501 (1) " When with my might." H., who puts comma after 2500.

2525 " Flee from a foot's length, the monster foe." H.

2538 (1) " Arose then by his shield." H.

2544 (1) " The fighter bold." H. Cf. 2201, 2351.

2545 (1) " He stood on stony arch." H., as parenthesis.

2566 (2) . . . " against the stout shield." H.

2570 (1) " Hastening forwards." H., after Müllenhoff; see H.'s
note.

2574-5 " Was to proceed as Weird did not permit,
(1) In battle renowned." H.

2577 (1) Text as H. G. says: " Perhaps, with Thorpe, to read,
' With the sword of Ing,' a king of the Danes." (See Additional Notes.)

2586 (2) . . . " That was no pleasant way." H.

2613 " To the friendless the vengeance of Weohstan the slayer.' H.

2638–41 (2) . . . " therefore he us chose

. . . .

To glory us urged, and gave me these treasures,
(1) Because he us deemed." H.

2660 (1) " Burnie and shield-sign." H.

2687 (1) " The wondrous-sharp weapon." H.

2765-66 (2) . . . " each one of mankind
Cause to be proud, guard himself he who will." H.
G. supplies *hord* = " hoard," in 2766 and takes *gehwone* =
" each" with it, but H.'s reading seems better. Ms. shows
no lacuna. W. as G.

2769 (1) " Wrought with link-work." H.

2777-79 (2) . . .; " the bill before felled

. . . .

Him who of these treasures." H., i.e., Beowulf's sword
killed the dragon, *ealdhláfordes* = " of the old lord," referring to Beowulf. See H.'s note.

2781 " Hot for the hoard, the fierce fighter-in air." H.

2792 (2) This half-line inserted by editors, though Ms. shows no omission.

2800 (2) . . . "ye" refers to Wiglaf alone.

2824 (1) "Helpless become." H.

2857 (2) . . . "with aught reverse." H. G. omits *wiht* = " aught," though contained in Ms.; both G. and H. insert *willan.*

2881 (2) . . . "the fire less strongly." H. W. as G. Z. as H.

2886 (1) "Possessions shall fail." H. *lufen = lufa;* cf. 1728.

2909 (1) "For the weary-in-thought." H., i.e., dead.

2930-32 Arnold thinks these lines "make no sense in their present context," and with line 2475, where *oððe* is changed to *þa þe,* should follow line 2478, but we cannot so emend "Beowulf," and his explanation of the incidents will not answer. See Glossary, s.v. Ongentheow.

2973 (1) "he," i.e., Ongentheow, and 2974 (1) " he," i.e., Wulf.

2977 (1) "The brave thane," i.e., Eofor, brother of Wulf.

2978 (1) "His own broad sword," H., as accus., which seems better. W. as H. Z. as G.

2984 H. puts period after this line; hence translate " Meanwhile " for " Whilst " in 2985.

2990 (1) " Gifts 'fore his people." H.

2994 (2) i.e., *sceattas* worth. Cf. 2195.

2995-6 For the long measure cf. 1162-68 and 1705-7.

3005 (2) Ms. *Scildingas,* but both G. and H. read *Scylfingas,* which makes better sense. Müllenhoff, however, thinks the line a mere thoughtless repetition of 2052; cf. H.'s note. *hwate Scylfingas* may be taken as parenthesis, referring back to 3001.

3030 (1) i.e., his predictions.

3041 (1) "The terrible stranger." H.

3056 (2) . . . "He is man's protector." H., as parenthesis.

3061 (1) " Some one of few." H., i.e., " some few."

3075 (1) "The Creator's favor," H., which is better, taking " he," 3074, as referring to Beowulf, with (:) after 3074 (1). Cf. H.'s note.

3084 (1) " We endured a hard fate:" H., with period after 3083.

3086 (1) " Which that ruler." H. Ms. shows no lacuna.

3104 (2) "That ye may enough see near at hand." H., after Gdtvg. and Bugge.

3129 (2) i.e., by no means did any one sorrow.

3150-56 Ms. much injured: translation according to G.'s emendations, but 3155 (1) and 3156 (1) are left blank by G. H. differs, but nothing to be made of the passage.

3161 (2) . . . " the best of flames." H. Ms. corrupt. W. as H.

THE FIGHT AT FINNSBURG.

1 (1) Emended by G.

5 (2) and 6 (1) added by G. to complete the sense. In 5 (1) H. has *fèr*, as in G.'s *Bibliothek*, hence " But assault bear forth."

12 (1) " Hold up your hands." H.

13 (1) " Fight ye in front." H.

14 (1) Added by G.

19 H. puts (;) after " himself," hence supply " he."

31 (2) " The keeled board should," H., i.e., the shield.

36 (1) " Wounded men tumbled." H. *lacra*, from *lâc* = " saucius " in G.'s Glossary to the *Bibliothek*: not given by H.

43 (1) " Bravely," and 44 (1) added by G. Omitted by W.

II.'s text varies but little from G.'s in the *Bibliothek*, whereas G., in his edition of "Beowulf," has made several emendations. H. omits in his Glossary several words, and all the proper names, peculiar to this fragment, even in his 4th edition. It lacks the care bestowed upon "Beowulf."

ADDITIONAL NOTES TO FINNSBURG.

22 Gdtvg. assumes lacuna of a half-line, and Rieger of a whole line, after 22. W.

26 Insert "quoth he" after "name." H. W. G.

43 Rieger inserts one line after 43, as follows :
    "(Warded off the Frisians, suffered distress.)" W. as H.

ADDITIONAL NOTES TO BEOWULF.

24 (1) "May lieges lead." H.

60 (2) W. reads *ræswa* as nom., referring to Heorogar. So Z.

62 W. reads "*þæt . . . wæs Onelan cwen*"; G.[8], "*þæt Onelan cwen . . . hatte.*" Ms. shows no lacuna between *þæt* and *elan.*

139 (2) W. inserts *rymde* = "rest for him prepared."

169 (1) "Before the Creator." G.[8]

181 (2) "The Lord God they knew not." H. W. G.[8]

240 (2) W. reads *hringedstefnan* = "the curvéd prow."

303(2)–305 W. reads, after Bugge, in 303 *Eofor lic-scionon* (dat. sing. of adj.), and in 305 *ferhwearde*, hence =
  . . . "The boar for the shining one
  . . . .
  . . . was keeping life-guard."

490 (1) W. as G., but G.[8] *sigehreð secgum* =
"The heroes, victorious one," i.e., Beowulf.

507 (2) . . . "in swimming contended." H. W. G.[8]

515–16 . . . "the sea welled with waves,
With winter's flood." H.

684 (1) "From sword refrain." H.

706 (2) Or, "since" for "whom."

707 (1) "The ceaseless foe." H. W. Cf. 801.

749 (2) i.e., Beowulf sat supported on his own arm. G. H.

801 (2) . . . "the ceaseless foe." H. W. Cf. 707.

897 (2) . . . "the worm hot melted." H. W.

900 (2) . . . (that he ere undertook). H.

902 (1) W. reads *earfoð* = "misery," but *eafoð* = "strength" is better.

1032 (1) *fêla lâfe* = "leavings of files," hence "swords." Ms. *laf.* Cf. 2829.

1107 (2) E. has given the best explanation of *icge.* He reads *ýcge*, and says: "*ýcg* (also *êcg, îcg*, is found) means *insula;* but gold of the island is dragon-gold, hoard-gold." For another example of *cg = g*, cf. Ms. 2893, *ecgclif = eg-clif.*

1135 (1) Lit. "those which ever observe," without (.). G. H. W.

1193 (2) i.e., gold wrought in the form of rings. Cf. 1382 and 3134.

1213 (,) after *guðsceare* and not after *léode.* H. (,) after 1212 and not in 1213. W.

1225 (1) " A happy prince." H.

1285 (1) i.e., "a sword inlaid with gold, or wound with gold-chains." G.

1320 (1) Lit. "in accordance with his courteous 'Good-night.'"

1363 (2) W. reads *hrîmge*, "rimy," for *hrînde*, Ms. and eds., = "dead." G.

1372 (2) ... "that's no secure place." H.

1488 (1) W. takes *Hunferð* as vocative ; hence, read "a" for second "the" in 1489.

1512 (1) "They harassed the hero." H.

1537 (2) ... "(shrank he not from the contest)." H.

1541 (2) ... "a reward repaid." H.

1604–5 Rather, "they neither knew nor thought that they were looking on their dear lord himself."

1616 (1) "The drawn sword burnt." H. So 1667.

1737 (2) ... "nor strife anywhere." H.

1807–8 (,) after "bear" and after "Ecglaf." H. (,) after "bear" but not after "Ecglaf." W.

1816 No punctuation mark after "man"; hence omit "he." W.

1894–5 *léodum*, H., W.; hence insert "to" after "welcome," and erase commas.

1923 (2) ... "there at home dwells." H.

1943 (1) "For insult assumed." H.

2029 (2) W. inserts *nô*, as H., and says that *nô* may have stood in the Ms. Z. says not.

2061 (1) i.e., having forfeited his life.

2157 W. as G., but Z. rightly reads *êst*, not *eft;* hence translate, "that I of his favor." H. does not insert *ôr* as G., but takes *ǣrest* as neut. subst. = "first condition."

2217–20 On this corrupt passage W. remarks : "The dragon could not avenge the theft, for he lay there put to sleep by the art [i.e., the magic art] of the servant."

2231 (1) "A vessel bright." W.

2275–6 W. as H. Z. supplies :
" Very much dread. He shall seek for
" The hoard in the earth."

2305 (1) " The evil one would." H., after Bugge, but contrary to Ms. G. adds *léoda*.

2361 "He alone thirty had on his arm." W. as G.[1] and Bugge.

2387 (2) Properly, grandson, i.e., Eadgils.

2456 (2) ... "the rest-place of winds." H.

2468 (2) ... " since woe him befell." H.

2521 (1) " His boasting cheek." G.   Text as H.

2523 (1) " Fierce heat oppressive." H. W. as G. Z. as H.

2576 (2) " Struck the frightfully bright one." H.

2577 *incgelafe* is one word in Ms., at beginning of a line.   Read *sinc-gelâfe* = "with the treasure-sword," i.e., precious or costly sword; *s* may have stood at end of 2576, and we might arrange : *slôh sinc-gelâfe, þæt sío ecg gewâc.* Cf. 2679 ; also *maððum-sweord*, 1023, *sinc-maððum*, 2193, and *sinc-gestréona*, 1226.   *gelâf* is not found, but many analogous forms exist, as *gelâc, gelâd, gestréon*, &c.   If this reading is correct, we need no longer seek an explanation for a hypothetical *incge*.

2619 (2) " his," i.e., Onela's.

2657 (1) Literally, " His old merits were not."

2698 (2) ... " when his kinsman he helped." H.

2869 (2) ... " such as anywhere best." H., referring to the armor.

3006 (1) *oððe* may be translated "and " here, as in 649 and 2475.   Cf. H.'s note to 647.

3062–65 H. gives Bugge's reading and explanation of this passage, which may be translated :

> ... " By a wondrous death
> Let a warlike earl the end then approach,
> Of his life-fate, when," &c.

3134 (1) Cf. note on 1193 (2).

3175 (1) " They highly extolled." H.

3181 (2) ... " of mighty kings." W.

www.ingramcontent.com/pod-product-compliance
Lightning Source LLC
Chambersburg PA
CBHW020016030726
47500CB00002B/617